THE INSATIABLE HUNGER OF TREES

SAMANTHA EATON

CONTENT WARNING

This book contains graphic depictions of victims killed by a supernatural creature, as well as the act of the creature hunting. There are graphic depictions of body horror including severe injury, physical mutation, self-harm, and gore. The main character's depression and disordered eating are prevalent throughout. Drug and alcohol use, as well as addiction, are mentioned. There are animal characters in this book, none of which are harmed or killed. Please proceed with caution if any of these subjects cause distress.

To anyone afraid to let go, even if it's the only thing you know to be right. You've got this.

ONE

People say the trees keep the secrets of killers, and so we fear them.

The forest surrounds me, no matter where I go in this county, and it taunts me with memories it will never share. It shields the people here from the worst crimes committed among the evergreens and aspens and maples, but woven within its branches, there is violence. The bare skeletons of deciduous trees whisper new tales to the needles of conifers, a language dead to humans.

They know what happened to my sister.

I listen to the winter birds cawing among the other sounds of the woods that circle the house where I watch foster kittens. Not the worst extracurricular, and it's a line on the resume that'll get me out of here one day. The birds' distant chatter fills my head and leaves no room for the content of the textbook I've been trying to read for hours.

A little monster of a kitten begs for my attention, pawing at the corners of pages and kneading the sleeve of my sweater from where she perches, predatory. She doesn't sense the presence I feel coming from the forest around us

—it isn't real yet—though every night, something invisible sends all four of them into hiding. Sends my skin into goosebumps. For now, Paisley plays, a black-and-white ball of fuzz hijacking the book in my lap in the last beam of sunlight before the light dies beneath the horizon.

"Paisley. Can you not?" I nudge the kitten off my book. "Go play with your pickle toy."

When the kittens first arrived in Minnesota after a long drive from Arizona in a carrier in Mel's Subaru, I was responsible for bottle feeding them and cleaning up their frequent messes. Now they think I'm a sentient climbing tower. At least this counts as volunteer work, and my boss at the supermarket says it'll look good when the time comes to pick candidates for the store's corporate internship and scholarship. She says it'll make me stand out to the important people at the company headquarters in St. Cloud. So, whatever. I do what I have to.

That'll be what they put on my gravestone when I die: "Cara Hughes: she did what she had to."

Paisley doesn't move, even after a second nudge. She digs her razor-sharp claws into my worn jeans, piercing the skin beneath the fabric.

I lean my head back until the crown of my skull touches the wall, then I exhale deeply. The sun outside turns the clouds a mix of yellow and pink against a darkening sky. Leafless tree limbs and the pointed tops of pines and spruces stand black against the last color they'll see until morning.

Soon, *it* will be here. Soon, the kittens will hide.

The trees watch over me like predators to prey. Uneasiness blooms in my bones, stronger and deeper since winter set in for good a few weeks ago. I can't shake it. It clings to me as desperately as Paisley clings to my jeans. Paranoia and fear and denial all blur together into a thick weight on my skin, lingering like the sting of a burn. And the trees keep promising that if I walk among them, I will find the thing I lost. The thing they took.

There are stories around here. They say there is a tree with the power to compel people to walk deep into the woods until they can't find their way out again. Local legend calls it the Winter Tree. Sometimes, its victims are found miles away in the same woods. Sometimes, state lines punctuate the distance between where they were lost and where they were found.

Other times, they vanish.

A lone crow caws loudly, somewhere else, and shatters the pull the woods have on me.

Shivers tear through my body, despite the warmth in this room.

I go to the window, hoping to find something more than the forest, but no animal-shaped shadows roam the backyard in search of an egg laid outside the coop by Laura the chicken. No hungry eyes peer at me from the brush. There are no wolves in Wolf County, but there are other things. Mel has had issues with predators in the past. Last summer, she lost all but one of her hens to a fox. The winter before that, she lost a cat to... *something*.

Tonight seems so much darker than the other nights this presence has come over me. No moons, no stars. No streetlights. All I can do is stare into the void my sister walked into a year ago and never returned from.

I still wonder what happened to Shelby when she lost sight of the place she entered the forest. For a while, I thought she'd come back for me. We'd always talked about leaving together, never about her going off alone. Did she lose her way? Did she come out the other side somewhere far away from here?

Did someone take her?

Nobody knows except her and the trees. They have centuries of secrets to keep, and none of us will ever convince them to share.

I leave the kittens' room to check out the other windows of the house for an animal skulking around. People around here love to talk, and, when the gossip runs dry, their favorite story to tell is the one where the roots of the forest swallowed my older sister whole after she left her truck parked by the mouth of an ATV trail. They say she stepped past the edge of the forest only to be devoured.

The problem is, nobody has any proof those stories are wrong.

Still, I'd give anything to rule them out as nothing more than conspiracies, so I look for something more believable. Dangerous animals exist out here, along with people worse than anything nature can conjure up—not that those answers make me feel any better.

Every window I look out shows me nothing but the dark barricade of the treeline.

My gut tells me to text Mel about the uncomfortable feeling that's been with me since the arrival of winter's shorter, darker days, but so far, I've resisted that urge. She'll think I'm being paranoid again, sinking back into worries that what took Shelby will take me next. I don't need her— a mentor I'd met while volunteering at the veterinary clinic in Riverside—thinking I'm falling back into the dark headspace I was in when Shelby first vanished.

Mel will be back from her night class to relieve me of my duty in about an hour anyway, and the ominous atmosphere will fade like it always does. So instead of bothering her, I lock the front door and go back to my attempts at studying.

When I return to the kittens' room, they're silent. If I didn't know better, I'd think they'd managed to get loose in the house.

Paisley sits alone at the window, pawing at the glass with ears alert. The other three kittens have hidden in the safety of their carpeted tower, little faces angled at the window in suspicion. Cats sense things. Not ghosts or spirits or demons—nothing like that. They catch changes in the atmosphere before a disaster, catch the threat of harm emanating from a stranger. Real things. Deadly things.

A chill rolls across my forearms and the hair at the back of my neck stands up straight.

"What do you see, little girl?" I whisper. Any louder, and I worry whatever she senses will find us here. "Is there somebody outside?"

Another bird calls out in the silence, much closer to the house than before. Paisley flinches at the noise but doesn't back down from her perch behind the safety of the glass. She flattens her ears against her head and hisses at the distant sound.

Then she bolts, diving beneath a fleece blanket tossed on the floor.

The chill in my body settles deeper.

I press my hands to the glass, looking for whatever frightened Paisley. Caught in the glow of the chicken coop's light, a figure moves. A creature much bigger than Laura the chicken, who doesn't venture outside when there's snow on the ground anyway.

At last, my eyes settle on the outline of something that doesn't belong.

A sick feeling appears at the very bottom of my stomach, and I swallow a hard lump that threatens to choke me.

The shadow doesn't look like any of the wildlife in this region. Too big to be a fox or raccoon, too upright to be a deer. It hunches over, almost like a person trying to escape being caught somewhere they shouldn't be—but the light casts shadows that distort its limbs. It stretches them and makes them appear thin and sick.

I blink.

The figure doesn't disappear.

It remains, still a shadow, and it rustles the brush as it hurries away.

How long has this thing been out there? Has it been watching me, or is it here for Mel?

Then, the silhouette dissolves into the darkness of the forest.

I stand frozen by the window, clutching the hem of my sweater in both hands in an attempt at comfort. If I keep watching, it might come back and step into the light, so I wait.

Like all the other nights I've spent staring out this window, I give up when the kittens emerge from their safe spaces. Whatever I saw out there has gone. I should feel better, but the feeling of being followed still lingers on the back of my neck.

Someone was watching me tonight. Just like they've been watching me every night for weeks.

I wonder if, one of these nights, they'll want to do more than watch.

TWO

I try, but I can't return to my studies. The thought of whoever was out there still lurking in the woods plagues me.

Outside, I hear movement. Footsteps on the front stairs. The locked doorknob being wiggled. A thud against the wood.

No, I'm getting worked up. Nobody's here.

The thud comes again, accompanied by a single knock.

I check the time on my phone. Eight fifteen. Mel's class doesn't end until eight thirty, then it's a half hour drive back from the high school where the community college holds its night classes. It's too early for her to be back.

The door groans open, and I bite my lip. I should have gone for the hunting rifle Mel keeps stashed behind all her coats. She taught me how to use it in case something like this happened, but that doesn't matter now.

Crap.

I hold my breath as the door closes behind whoever came in.

All logic flies out of my head.

"Cara?" Mel's smooth voice floats over the jingling of her service dog's collar.I exhale and my heart sinks back to where it belongs. "Why was the door locked?"

I exhale and my heart sinks back to where it belongs.

My pulse races, burning off the last of the adrenaline from the moments before I knew the intruder wasn't an intruder at all.

Instead of going to greet her, I deflate against the wall in exhaustion. Paisley and another kitten, Checker, take the opportunity to crawl up my sleeves to my shoulders one last time before I leave for the night.

"Hey, class got done early." Mel slips into the kitten room without the dog, Hope, who's been trained well enough to be fine with the cats. It's Paisley and her claws we have to worry about, so the pit bull mix stays patiently on the other side of the door.

"Oh. Cool."

"Why'd you lock the door?" she asks. Despite the prevalence of carefully stored firearms, nobody locks their doors around here. Maybe they should start.

I shrug. "I got the creeps. It's nothing."

She accepts my lack of explanation. "Well, I still have my boots on if you want me to go start your truck. It's, like, a single degree outside."

I try not to let her see the flood of relief that washes over me when I fish my keys out of the front pocket of my bag. If it means not thinking about people creeping around in the woods, I'll take the charity.

In the kitchen, I make myself look busy trying to fit all my books in my too-old backpack while she ventures outside again.

From the corner of my eye, the truck's lights catch my attention. In their yellow glare, Mel's outline comes back toward the house. My imagination tricks me into thinking a second figure walks with her, a few feet back, and my heart stammers again. A jolt of panic hits me straight in the center of my chest, and I look for the dog.

Hope stands by the door, tail wagging slightly. If she can sense Mel's low blood sugar level by smelling her breath, surely she'd notice if there were anything really out there.

"It's real weird out there tonight," Mel says when she returns. "Coyote's probably back."

I nod, then glance at the dog. By looks, she could be a guard dog. Beefy, muscular body. Boxy gray head. Cropped ears. One look might deter someone from crossing her, but there's a reason she's a diabetic alert dog and not a security system. She has the warm and sweet personality of a loaf of raisin bread.

"Will you lock the door tonight?" I ask. It'll make me feel better. "The cats were acting weird. Paisley hissed at the window."

Mel chuckles as she fixes her night-sky-black hair into a bun atop her head, exposing the thistles tattooed up the brown skin of her neck. "Paisley is unreliable. She probably saw her reflection."

"Nah, the other three hid for a while too."

"I'll lock it. Okay?" She turns to rummage through her fridge like she hasn't eaten in weeks, and returns with a glass dish of lasagna and a bottle of light beer. "Hungry? It's butternut squash and spinach."

She pops the dish in the microwave without waiting for my answer. I decline anyway, though the lasagna sounds delicious.

She means well, repeatedly telling me to help myself to whatever's in the fridge, but I never take anything. I don't like the idea of anyone thinking I need help. Or worse, sympathy.

"I have to head home. I still have a history quiz to study for. Didn't get much done tonight..." I let the sentence die on my lips, the uneasy feeling crawling back over me.

"You could probably cut back on the hours for a bit now that this litter's a bit older. Take a break before things get busy in the spring." She takes her lasagna from the microwave, dropping the dish suddenly on the counter when the hot glass burns her finger. She pops the injured finger in her mouth to soothe it, and digs around the utensil drawer with the other hand for a fork. "When we get another litter that needs more constant care, you can ramp up your time here again."

She adds the last part probably because my face drops at the thought of not coming here. I like the cats. I like feeling like I have a little control over something good.

"I'll be okay. It's good for me to get out of the house."

"All right then. Just tell me if you need a break, okay? I need to be able to count on you come March."

"You can."

I hoist my backpack over one shoulder and groan at the weight, then tell Mel I'll see her in a couple days.

"Say hi to Charlie for me!" She grins at the mention of the cat she insisted I adopt back when I helped at the clinic.

"Bold of you to assume she's awake. Ever."

I tug on the wool knit hat my grandma made me a few Christmases ago before she died, then I brace for the cold. Even though I'll only be outside for a second, the thought of cold air biting my skin gives me chills before I leave the warmth of Mel's kitchen. The universe royally screwed up when it stuck me in Minnesota.

The air gnaws on my exposed cheeks and nose on the

way to the truck, and I hope the heat in the old Dodge has decided to kick in inside the cab.

It hasn't.

The truck has reached a temperature barely warmer than outside, and it leaves me longing for the constant, comfortable seventy-two degrees of the kittens' room.

I smack the dashboard above the vents as if that'll make the heat work.

Sometimes, I understand why Shelby would have walked into these woods just to throw everyone off her trail so she could escape to a place like Los Angeles or Vegas. Or somewhere off the beaten path like Tucson or Albuquerque. Someplace warm and civilized and full of people, unlike the scattered towns of Wolf County. Out here, I see more animals than people, and the highlight of regional events are things like harvest festivals and that one corn maze an hour away that made it onto some popular travel blog.

Even if there were more than two notable things to do, the cold ruins it. What's fun about getting lost in the corn when you can't feel your face?

I like to think she found a place where she felt right. Then I can stop worrying that her body will be recovered by a hiker or hunter when the snow thaws again. That's what the police say will happen if anything. Her case has been a recovery, not a rescue, for eight months.

A light in the trees catches my attention, and pulls it from Shelby, back into the present. The usually round reflection of animal eyes blur, almost liquid, and I can't comprehend the height of it. Nothing stands that tall around here. Not even the moose.

I blink a few times to clear my vision, but the red orbs stay where they are. Too high. Too bright. Too wrong.

Maybe... maybe someone stuck some of those mailbox

reflectors really high. People get bored and do shit like that all the time.

Or, I think cougars climb.

Another car approaches and I turn off my brights as it passes, then glance back at the reflections. They follow me, moving between the trees, and I press a little harder on the gas in hopes of losing them.

My lights catch a figure filling the space between trees. Upright like a man, but too tall, too thin.

My mouth turns to sandpaper at the sight, and I want to go faster but I can't risk it. Fifty miles per hour is enough. Any more and the curves will kill me if a patch of ice doesn't.

Ahead, another red light. This one blinks. It takes me a second to realize this one belongs. It indicates the intersection of the two roads leading from Montville to Wolf Hill and tells me to stop. Instead, I speed up.

I enter the intersection at the exact moment something else steps from the forest onto the pavement.

In the space between heartbeats, my truck meets the solid body of something large, something alive. Everything moves so fast, I don't get a good look at what I hit, but it definitely isn't human.

Hair or fur bursts up into view in my headlights. Then, a blur of limbs struggling to right themselves. Arms or legs flail for something to hold. The figure's eyes glow red across the darkness before it disappears beneath my line of sight.

I ease off the gas and hit the brakes, and something hard drags against the truck's door with a chilling screech. My stomach turns as it drags on, impossibly loud in the silence.

My truck sputters from the impact, and I worry it will stall on me.

"Please, no." I step harder on the gas, my pulse like double bass drums inside my ears. "Come on."

Gaining distance, I check the rearview mirror. A mangled heap lies motionless on the road.

I should stop. I should see what I hit.

A lump forms in my throat, and I swallow hard. I won't stop.

I press the accelerator again, and this time the truck picks up speed. As I drive away, I ignore the urge to look back. Even when the shrill scream of a dying creature breaks the night into a thousand jagged pieces.

THREE

People rush past me in the school parking lot while I stand beside my truck, hands on my hips, inspecting the scratches in the driver's side door. Last night, I'd rushed into the house without thinking about the damage, and I left this morning while it was still dark. Until now, I haven't had the chance to look at the truck, and now I can't tear my eyes away from the deep grooves in the metal.

They look like claw marks, like the edgy decals people stick on their muscle cars to look tough—except these are real. They've cut so deep, pale metal contrasts with the matte black paint on top.

Shelby would be pissed to see her truck like this.

"What happened here?"

My eyes roll as far back into my head as possible. Lucas Powell. My least favorite person in the whole entire school. Granted, Wolf County regional doesn't have thousands of students to choose from. Even if it did, Lucas would still be the worst.

You'd think we'd commiserate—me with my missing

sister and him with his tragically dead dad—but we absolutely do not.

I turn to him, arms crossed, and scowl. "I don't have time for your conspiracy theories today," I say.

Lucas Powell believes in monsters.

"What made those marks then?" He shrinks beneath my glare, despite him being a good eight inches taller than me.

"I..." Why do I default to explaining myself? I don't owe him an explanation. "Who cares? People hit shit all the time around here."

"Nothing that'd make that mark." He makes too much eye contact when he speaks, dark eyes locking on mine as if he thinks he'll win me over if he looks hard enough. "What has a paw that big?"

He mirrors my posture and crosses his arms, but it looks more like an act of protecting his vulnerable organs than one of defiance. I guess he has reason enough to be uncomfortable.

Last time we talked, he suggested Sasquatch took Shelby.

Okay, I don't know if it was Sasquatch exactly, but it was a monster. I remember the rage burning through my body like fire devouring a trail of gasoline. Whether he'd suggested Bigfoot or the Devil or the goddamn Easter Bunny, I would have had the same reaction. It was two days after she disappeared. My sister hadn't even been gone for forty-eight hours, the police didn't have a theory yet—but Lucas did. Cryptids.

He ended up in the search party with me and my girlfriend, Marie, in the woods. Everyone else was so much older, and exhaustion had wiped my ability to think straight off the table. My priority wasn't avoiding Lucas, the kid who openly believes the supernatural killed his dad. It was finding some sign of my sister.

Between whispers of "what a shame, that poor girl," Lucas made his suggestion.

"There are things around here, you know," he said. "One of them could have taken her." He said it like Bigfoot exists in the same way murderers and kidnappers exist. In the same way accidents exist. He acted like Shelby being taken by a monster was inevitable because our woods have a reputation.

And he said it after I'd been awake all night, searching her room for hints of a planned departure.

When people vanish in movies, there's always a journal hidden under the mattress with an elaborate plan. I was desperate to find it. It had to be there.

Shelby had to have left on purpose.

She wasn't dead. I refused to believe that. Even if her room had no secret notebooks, no typed goodbye left open on an abandoned laptop, she wasn't dead.

I told him to shut up. Marie tried to get him to go walk with an older couple nearby. Lucas kept talking, spouting theories as if they made anyone but him feel better about the situation.

My fist hit his stomach with a thud, cutting him off mid-syllable. He toppled backward, fell through the frozen surface of a shallow brook, and hit his head on a rock.

I had never hit anyone before that, and haven't since. I've always been more of a pacifist, an avoider. Every time I see him, as much as I despise him, I wish I could take it back.

"Why are you still standing here?" I ask.

He glances away from me for the briefest second, and I think he might consider trying again to convince me that his monsters are real. But he doesn't. He swallows the words instead.

"Sorry. Just thinking about what it could have been. A bear, maybe?" Lucas, of all people, should know the bears are hibernating. Someone whose family makes a living hunting and tracking predator animals would know nothing local to this area made those marks on my truck. "I'm, uh … I'm glad you didn't get hurt."

He waits a beat before leaving me standing alone. I glance once more at the scratches and trace them with my own hand. Spread all the way, my fingers still don't reach far enough to make such a big mark. Bears though, have big paws. Especially grizzlies, though I'm not sure we have those around here.

I accept the explanation for now, even if it doesn't sit right. It makes more sense than a cougar or a person.

Inside the school, tension hangs in the air. Where voices usually compete with one another to be heard, there are whispers. Hushed voices share secrets loud enough only for the intended recipient. Everyone else gets left to their own conversations, cut out of the full story creating the mood in the hall.

Lucas stands with a group of other seniors and I accidentally make eye contact with him as I pass. His friends follow his gaze until their eyes fall on me too, and I wish I could shake them off. One of his companions stares a bit harder, a bit more invested in my presence than the rest like she thinks the apology I owe her might appear out of thin air.

I avoid the eyes of my now ex-girlfriend, Marie, with more effort than I have to offer.

"Hey Cara," she says.

Her voice makes me freeze.

Sometime in the months after Shelby left, Marie stopped trying to get through to me. Her voicemails turned to missed calls she gave up on after a few rings, and those turned into texts that grew shorter and shorter until eventually, she gave up on me.

The guilt of shutting her out still hangs on me, but I had no choice. I can't lose anyone else the way I lost my sister, my best friend. I'd rather be alone than feel that hopelessness again.

"Hi," I say.

"Did you hear about Saturday's party?" she asks.

"Uh, no. Who would have ...?" *Bite your tongue, Cara. Don't be sarcastic.* "No."

This time, Lucas speaks up. "I know you don't want to hear about this stuff, but listen ..." He holds up his hands as if they can either prevent me from leaving or from tearing into him. "Some kids had a party at someone's family cabin. People were going to make the hike to the Winter Tree and carve their initials into it."

Of course they were. Messing with a reportedly possessed tree is this town's favorite pastime. It's the only thing of interest on the entire county's Tripadvisor page. People make day trips from Duluth or Minneapolis or Fargo to leave their names in the bark, then go home with stories of how they survived Wolf County's local legend.

"Before they even left the cabin, a bunch of them saw something weird. I know you don't believe in this stuff but I think it's worth considering. It could explain the scratches on your truck."

Marie's eyes widen at the mention of damage to my truck.

"Lucas... please. Don't."

"I know. I know. Just, keep it in mind. It could be dangerous."

"You said it yourself, it was probably a bear."

He frowns. "Listen, I'm sorry about the search party. I shouldn't have said what I did."

Every word sets me on edge. I keep my eyes fixed on my scuffed boots and pick at the skin beside my pinky nail, drawing a tiny bead of blood that blooms into a thin stream down my fingertip.

"But I still think there is something here we need to be afraid of." Lucas's rambling finally ends.

"I saw it too," Marie says.

The warning bell rings above us. Five minutes until class starts. I don't have time for this conversation; it needs to end.

"You believe this stuff now?"

She nods, straight black hair falling loosely over her shoulders.

"What did it look like?" I ask though I don't care what it looks like. What I care about is how she, of all people, went to a cabin party. She hated them more than I did. Hated the way people always drank too much and staggered out into the cold.

Then, I notice the fingers of her left hand laced with those of the girl standing next to her. She, unlike me, has finally decided to move on. I should be happy for her, but instead, my stomach goes rancid with jealousy.

I have no right to feel this way.

But here I am. Jealous. Jealous of this girl for getting the warmth of Marie's soft hands. Jealous that everyone else gets to move on, but I can't so much as look at the forest without wondering what it hides.

Marie doesn't notice me staring at her hand though, and puts together an answer to my question after thinking for a minute. "I thought it might be an animal at first, but it appeared to be a biped. And it was skinny. Like, really skinny, you know? Uh, you know… kind of like the Slenderman. Like that. And it was taller than the shed. I don't know what it was but lots of people saw it. Cassandra saw it too."

The girl beside her nods. "It stared at us for a long time," Cassandra says in a low, calm voice. "It had these terrible eyes. I'm pretty sure it was a demon. It—"

"Okay." I don't need Marie and her new girlfriend nagging me about monsters too. "Well, I didn't see anything like that." I turn back to Lucas. "Like I said, I don't know what I hit, and I really don't care."

FOUR

The cabin smelled like a mix of pine and stale cigarette smoke, much heavier on the latter because apparently some kids still thought smoking was a badass thing to do. Or, maybe vaping just hadn't caught on in Wolf County yet. Realistically, the trend had another couple years before it found us, one last civilization untouched by root beer scented vapor.

Shelby convinced me to come to the party since Marie was visiting her grandparents in Seoul, and, at the time of the negotiation, I thought it might be better than being at home bored. So far, it wasn't.

I sat, picking at a loose thread on the old couch that could only be described as Christmas plaid—red and green and brown and atrociously ugly—while Shelby dealt with an already drunk Emily. My sister's best friend had only recently found out that her boyfriend, who was a freshman at some college in Milwaukee, cheated on her. A lot. So

Shelby had to abandon her duty of looking out for me in favor of making sure Emily didn't wander out into the woods alone. Or worse, call the boyfriend and make a fool out of herself. Priorities.

A weight appeared on the couch beside me, plopping down on one side of my cushion with such force it raised me up a bit. "Sorry Cara," Parker, Shelby's I-guess-boyfriend, said as a wave of yellow liquid spilled over the edge of his metal camp mug and onto the toe of my boot.

Parker took a sip of his beer, then held a still sealed can of something out to me. "Pepsi?" he asked.

I didn't really feel like it. Didn't want the fuzzy layer of sugar to collect over my teeth for the rest of the night, but the caffeine called to me. I'd wanted to go to bed hours ago, and I still had to drive Shelby and Emily home, so I accepted the pop.

Over in the corner by the fireplace, a group of girls started laughing and cheering while one of them stabbed a hole in the bottom of a can with a pocket knife and pressed it to her mouth as the liquid sprayed. Shelby. Then a second cheer echoed the first, and Emily gulped down her beer too.

"Parker, I'm gonna need help with them," I said. "Can you convince them to get in the car?"

Parker rose, and my couch cushion deflated beneath me again.

Alone, I opened the can of pop and drank it for the sake of having something to do while Parker wrangled Emily and Shelby into the truck. Cabin parties were always like this. Someone always wound up drinking too much or got too sad. If I was lucky, Shelby would at least hold off on puking until I got her home.

The Pepsi was too sweet, but I kept drinking from the

can. Bored. If Emily hadn't gotten upset, the four of us could've finished our slightly less boring game of Parcheesi —because that's the kind of game people with hunting cabins keep under the stairs. I had almost won. One of my two remaining pawns was already in my safe zone, and the other was only a few spaces away. Locked behind Shelby's blockade, of course. My sister liked playing dirty, or at least being a pain in my ass whenever she could, but I guess at least we didn't hate one another like some sisters do.

Of course, Emily's sadness gave Shelby the opportunity to let loose in the name of being a good friend.

"We should go find the tree!" Emily's slurred voice rang out over the rest of the noise in the small cabin. "Let's go!"

I rolled my eyes.

"No, Emily. You're going home." Parker's voice was patient as he steered Emily away from the back door.

Knowing a half-drunk Parker would need help with the two girls, I left my soda beside the Parcheesi board and rose to cross the room. As expected, Shelby broke away from the small group and swayed as she stood by the window.

"But it's haunted, Parker. Don't you want to see? Come with us," Shelby protested. "It'll be so *cooool.*" The last word dragged on too long.

I stepped between my sister and the door leading out to the forest. "We can go see it another time. I promise."

My sister glanced at me, eyes closing in an out-of-sync blink. She was drunk enough now that she'd probably forget the promise by morning, like I hoped. Promises were legally binding, as far as Shelby was concerned.

"I want to go now." Emily stomped, then let herself drop to a sitting position on the ground. Wasted, she acted like a toddler denied a candy bar at the grocery store.

"Cara, I don't want to go home. This party is fun. Emily needs this. Home is so boring," Shelby whined.

"Home isn't boring. Home is where you get to sleep off all that beer you drank."

Shelby blinked again, then looked at me with a blank stare. "I didn't drink beer, I drank cider."

"Great. You can sleep off all your cider and hope you're not too hungover to drive me to work tomorrow." Impatience slipped into my voice, but she didn't notice.

Parker and I led Shelby and Emily to the truck, and he lifted them both in—Shelby first in the middle seat where the center console flips up, and Emily in the passenger's seat. He even buckled their seatbelts, though it took a few times in his state.

"You going to be okay getting out?" Parker asked.

"I'll be fine."

The truck was silent while I figured out how to turn around among the scattered trees and other vehicles. The faint sound of snoring came from the passenger's seat, suggesting Emily had passed out from however much she drank. Shelby and Emily combined smelled like they'd washed their clothes in beer, and the faint odor of cigarettes came off the fabric of the flannel Shelby had taken from Parker.

"That was fun," Shelby slurred. Her voice shook from the bumps in the road.

"What if we did literally anything else next time? Doesn't Emily have a Switch at her house? We could go play Mario Kart or something."

The lights on the dashboard barely illuminated Shelby's expression, but I still saw it.

"Ugh. They'll have a Switch in my retirement home."

I didn't say anything else, because I should've known

she'd say something like that. Shelby liked the illusion of nightlife created by Parker's cabin parties. She liked the drama of Emily's meltdowns. And she wanted me to like those things too when all I wanted was to play a full round of Parcheesi.

FIVE

My boss, Anna, sends me a text asking me to come to work for a few hours after school, a welcome distraction after a day of obsessing over bears. The monotony of work will pull out of my head, sparing me from thoughts of Marie and her new girlfriend doing all the things she and I used to do together.

I shouldn't be jealous. I cut her out of my life like a dying organ. Still, the envy creeps in.

At the supermarket, I pull on my butter yellow polo over the long-sleeve black shirt I wore to school, tie my chin-length brown waves into a ponytail, and head for the breakroom to punch in. With one hand over the punch button and the other on my phone, I start my shift while finishing a text to Mom so she knows where I am. She'll worry otherwise.

Nice-N-Spice, a proud, Minnesotan supermarket chain, is made up of outrageously bad taglines on weekly flyers —*Nice deals to spice up your meals!!!*—and the smiling salt and pepper shakers the designers used for the *I*s in the name. A girl like me can fade into the background behind the tacky, brightly colored things meant to catch customers' eyes.

"Cara, can you log in on seven? Mike hasn't had a break yet, Decker called out, and Jilly's going home. We're gonna be short-staffed for a few minutes." Anna barks her orders as I approach the front-end. "Glad you could make it in. I can always count on you."

I offer a polite smile and shrug. Operating short-staffed is something I've gotten used to here. Anna likes to blame it on "lazy kids these days who don't want to work." She says it in front of me like I'm an exception to that rule. Like, despite being a kid, I have reached a point of superiority over others because I show up on time and don't call in sick. Because I have nothing better to do, she calls me the reliable one in front of the others, and I hate it. If I weren't depending on the summer internship in St. Cloud and its sponsored two-year degree, I'd find somewhere else to work.

But I can't afford college without the help, so I pretend Anna's comments don't make me uncomfortable.

As I flip on the light above my register, an older couple pushes their cart down my lane. I recognize the pair as two of our regulars, Ellen and Roger Howe. Ellen always shows up with a half filled-out check, and Roger comes with jokes.

The two of them are nice. Neither of them asks questions about Shelby. They let me grieve without reliving the loss, unlike most people in this town who thrive on gossip. Ellen prefers to know what kind of "bizarre fruit" we have in stock and whether I've tried it. Usually, I have not.

"We have the star fruit again," I say as she approaches the register.

She puckers her lips. "Not that again. It was bitter."

I chuckle, though my laughter always sounds so forced, and focus on scanning their items.

"Not as bad as those kumquats the kid in produce made me get last month. If I wanted to eat orange peel, I'd buy an orange. Cheaper that way, too."

I flick my eyes up to Ellen's icy blue ones to find the laughter she holds in them, then keep working through her order. Every now and then, I pick up something that makes Roger perk up. He jokes about how he's not allowed to buy jerky unless he cleans the wood stove, so he's stopped using it in an effort to keep it pristine.

"You know," Ellen says, "my grandson said people saw Bigfoot."

"Oh?" I say, not really paying attention.

She shakes her head. "I told him a gorilla probably escaped the zoo. Bigfoot isn't stupid enough to be caught by a couple drunk kids in the woods."

"Really, Ellen? You're on this monster kick too?" I force the dryness from my voice.

She shoots me a wicked grin. "I haven't traveled the world. I don't know all the creatures who live in it."

"Okay. Fine."

I tell her the total, steering away from talk of Bigfoot, and she scrawls it onto the empty space on her check before handing it over. Our interaction ends with a thank-you, and the next customers come through—one after another— until I lose track.

Some time passes before someone catches my eye at the end of the baking aisle. She looks around as though she's lost someone. Her bright white hair stands out under the unflattering light, and her posture is familiar. I'd know the stance anywhere. Her stance carries an effortless confidence—not too cocky, but not someone to be trifled with—with one hand on her hip and the other fiddling with a lock of hair.

The girl's presence hits me somewhere deep, because it isn't who I think it is. My sister wouldn't come back here, not after this long.

She got me this job as soon as I was old enough to work, and we worked the same shifts so we could drive together. She'd take cashier duty and I'd bag, treating each order like a game of grocery store Tetris. On slow days, I'd wipe down the register with disinfectant while she'd stand at the end of the aisle in hopes of finding someone ready to check out. She always stood the way this girl stands now, one hand on her hip and the other busy. It made people want to come to our lane and talk to her.

Sometimes I think it would be better if I were the one who'd gone missing.

As much as I know the girl standing in my store isn't my sister, I want to believe it. If it were her, it would be the end of this nightmare that is losing her. If it were her, I would no longer be stuck between being a girl with a sister and a girl without.

I close my eyes, then walk my customer through using the new chip reader to process his credit card.

My sister is not here.

She didn't come back for me.

With my line of customers gone for now, I find a roll of paper towels under the register and wipe down the conveyor belts and focus too intently on the task. It keeps me from looking for the girl I saw, from finding the spot she once occupied to be empty.

When I look up, she's gone.

I could swear it was her, even though she didn't look for me where she knew she'd find me, working the cash register. I shouldn't get my hopes up. Shelby would have said something to me, or she wouldn't have come here at all.

SIX

Alight snow falls in slow motion from the sky when I step into the parking lot, and I pull my jacket tighter around my body. Fortunately, the snow doesn't stick when it hits the pavement, so the twenty-minute drive home should be uneventful.

As I wipe slush off my windshield with a sleeve, I look around the parking lot for signs of the girl I saw earlier. The liquid seeps in through the thin fabric of my shirt and sends frost through my veins. A couple storms ago, I broke the cheap scraper Shelby kept by the passenger's seat, and I haven't replaced it. The lime green, four-dollar scraper sits in two pieces on the floor, another reminder of my sister I can't bring myself to discard.

I wish I found the nerve to speak up, to call my sister's name and see if the girl responded, but I couldn't do it.

The whole way home, I think about Shelby and where she might be, what she might be doing. I won't let myself imagine her dead, so I make up different scenarios. Even in a house that hasn't seen her in over a year, signs of her exis-tence remain. A size-eight outline of melted snow and salt stains the unfinished, plywood floor by the door where she'd once kept her favorite pair of boots.

Everyone's so afraid to fill her place because they're hell-bent on believing she'll come back and fill it herself.

From the kitchen comes warmth and the sound of one of my parents clanging dishes against one another in the sink. The fan above the stove rattles, and I smell garlic. I'd almost forgotten today is Tuesday, the only day Dad has off from the hospital, so the only day the three of us eat together.

"Hey," I say as I step into the kitchen.

Mom turns from where she stands at the sink, dries her hands on a towel. "Hi Cara. Dinner's almost done. I'm just waiting on your dad to get back with some spaghetti."

"I could've grabbed a box." She knows I got called in, but doesn't like to ask me for help. She doesn't think she needs it.

"I guess I didn't think of that."

I grab the towel off the stove and dry some of the dishes Mom already washed. You'd think, after a lifetime of it, I'd be used to the clutter in this house, but it makes me feel like the walls are closing in. The claustrophobia isn't just from the piles of dishes stacked by the sink or the laundry heaped on the couch where it will sit until someone has a minute to fold it. This house should be big enough for us now. Mom and Dad should be able to move their bed out of the living room and into the one that used to belong to Shelby, but they won't. She might come back. She'll need a place to sleep.

"How was school?" Mom asks.

"Fine."

She knows I ditched all my friends and stopped talking to people months ago, and she must know it hasn't changed. We never talked about it, really, but she knows better than to ask. She knows she'll either get a lie or a half-assed version of the truth.

With the conversation dead, the sound of sauce bubbling on the stovetop swallows the kitchen. At least for a few minutes before the door groans open and Dad comes inside. He's better at getting information out of me because he always asks me questions I can't answer with one word. I guess he learned that from years of asking patients, *What's wrong, what hurts?*

The difference between his patients and me? They have something to get better from. They need fixing.

I don't.

"What happened to your truck?" is the question Dad opens with.

Mom's eyes bulge.

"Did you get in an accident? Did someone hit you? Is someone bothering you at school?" The possibilities tear through Mom's head like wildfire. "Was it that Lucas kid?"

"It looks like someone dragged a pitchfork down the door," Dad says.

"Oh my god." Mom puts a hand, holding the half-open box of pasta Dad bought, to her mouth. "When did this happen?"

"It's not a big deal. I hit a bear or something on my way back from Mel's last night." Lucas's lie ends up being good for something after all.

Mom goes gray.

Dad frowns. He doesn't believe me. "A bear?" he asks. "Are you sure?"

"No, I'm not sure. But I definitely wasn't getting out to look."

Mom pours the pasta into a pot of boiling water, lips

pursed and movements stiff. She doesn't look at me—not because she's angry, but because she doesn't want to break.

"It's fine," I say. "I'm okay. The truck's okay. Everything is okay."

Reassuring her comes naturally now. At this point, reassuring her comes before anything else.

AFTER DINNER, I retreat to my room to work on my homework. Somewhere in the middle of the chapter I have to read for biology, I fall asleep with the book in my lap and my neck bent at an odd angle.

Charlie, my cat, wakes me when she moves out from her favorite spot beneath my comforter too fast and knocks the textbook to the floor. When my eyes adjust to being awake, I find her at the window with her front paws on the chipped paint of the wooden sill. Her ocean-green eyes fixate on something in the woods, and the tip of her tail twitches.

"What is it, Charl?"

She ignores me.

"Charlie. Hey," I say, firmer this time.

A chill from the poorly insulated window settles deep in my bones, and I pull a quilt around my shoulders. The cat stops purring, and growls instead.

Two familiar red orbs stand out in the curtain of darkness, glowing.

In the time it takes—mere seconds—to find my phone and use the sliver of reception I have to search what color bears' eyes glow in the light, the eyes disappear.

All night, I think about those orbs. I trick myself into thinking I see them everywhere. In the woods. In the yard.

In my room. Something invisible tracks every movement I make. It waits for an opportunity... to what? To attack? To steal me away into the woods? I don't know what this is.

Exhaustion cranks my senses into overdrive and makes me hear things clearer. A door opening and closing. The refrigerator door smacking the counter when it swings open too far. Water pouring from the tap. A chair's legs being dragged across the floor.

Charlie perks up again.

Maybe Dad couldn't sleep since he's used to being up all night. Or maybe Mom's anxiety settled in after hearing about my truck.

People's monster stories sneak in through my ears and make their home in my head where they've never been welcome. Thoughts of malevolent beings taller than anything I've ever seen, with claws and teeth like knives plague my head.

I do not believe in monsters.

I do not believe.

Still, I swing my legs over the edge of the bed and head down the hall to the kitchen for a glass of water and to see who's awake.

The old floorboards creak beneath my weight and give away my presence to whoever turned the kitchen light on. I wouldn't be surprised to find Mom at the table with a cup of tea cradled in her hands, eyes red from exhaustion or stress or both. Sometimes, she gets so overwhelmed, I find her here in the morning, passed out over her laptop and piles of bills. I've offered to help, to relinquish some of my pay from the supermarket to cover electric or heat. She and Dad never accept, too prideful to let their seventeen-year-old daughter carry some of the weight anchoring us to a life of never having quite enough.

But instead of Mom, I find someone else in the kitchen. A ghost of someone I only expect to find in memories, in the empty places she used to be when I get tired enough to believe the lingering hope buried deep.

The apparition has hair the color of fresh snow. Pale skin contrasts with dark makeup around her eyes, smudged at the edges from days of wear. It looks like her, looks like the girl I saw at the supermarket.

It even sits like her, huddled in the chair with her chin on folded knees.

Trees outside dance in the wind, their branches creating a symphony of sound in the otherwise dead silence of the night. Harsh gusts whistle against the sides of the house, and it feels like they tear through me too.

My breathing goes shallow. There is not enough air in this house for me.

I fold my arms over my stomach to fight the ball of worry growing inside me, then I force my mouth and tongue to form the shape of her name.

Three attempts and it finally passes my lips, no more than a whisper.

"Shelby?"

SEVEN

Something almost hard struck me between the shoulder blades, and my body tensed up. The sound of the object hitting the ground behind me was muffled by raucous laughter. Shelby. Shelby threw an apple at me.

When I turned, she held another. She tossed the browned, probably wormy red delicious apple in the air and caught it again.

"I finally found a use for these," Shelby said, grinning.

Red delicious apples were, in fact, the least delicious of all apples.

A wicked grin spread across her face as she faked throwing the apple at me. The mischief in it reached her eyes, and I could swear they glittered when she acted like this. I always thought, when we got old, Shelby would have the best stories. I'd be the boring one who lived for safety and comfort instead of clutching the last shreds of wild animal left in our DNA.

"Don't," I said.

Shelby wound up for a throw, and I put my hands up.

"Stop." I couldn't keep myself from laughing, though I wanted to be mad.

She'd dragged me out apple-picking when she knew I had a presentation to give that day, a presentation I'd been preparing to give for three weeks. Missing it made me itchy, but Shelby wouldn't have understood if I'd asked her to turn around and drop me at the school. She wouldn't have understood if I said I didn't want to go.

I didn't say no to Shelby.

I don't think she'd have recognized the word on my lips even if I'd tried.

The apple soared through the air, and I ran. I weaved through the rows of macintosh and granny smith trees, dodging the flying fruit Shelby sent my way.

She cornered me at the edge of the property, a wild look in her eyes.

"Do you surrender? You should. You're unarmed."

Another apple struck my hip. Juice squirted from the fruit where the skin burst on contact, leaving a sticky smear on my sweater.

"You're going to get us kicked out." I held up my hands in defeat.

She laughed, but didn't pick up another apple. "Fine."

We filled our bags with the prettiest fruits we could find, then shared an order of apple cider donuts from the store by the entrance.

When we finished, Shelby drove to the corn maze half an hour away. It was vacant in the middle of the day on a Wednesday, so we had the place to ourselves. We got lost in the tall stalks, eating fried Oreos as we wandered.

"We already went that way," I said as Shelby made a left turn we'd tried twice already.

"Oh." She pivoted on her feet, out of balance. "This way then."

She led the way, stopping now and then to drink from a bottle of Pepsi that somehow never got emptier. With each sip, her movements became less sturdy, and she sometimes wobbled enough to try using the corn to catch her balance.

In the middle of the maze, she set the empty Pepsi bottle on a hay bale beside a scarecrow and reached into her jacket and retrieved a cheap, plastic flask.

I shouldn't have been surprised. I should have figured out why she'd gotten increasingly silly as we wandered. The wonder of being lost in an acre of corn didn't work the way it had when we were young.

"Want some?" Based on the sound of liquid sloshing in the flask, it was nearly empty. "Actually, no. Wait. I need you to drive. Will you drive home?"

Without a choice, I took her keys. I wish I had taken the flask too, but she wandered off with it before I could.

By the time we reached the end of the maze, Shelby hadn't stopped giggling for ten minutes and had talked herself into needing chili fries from the truck stop diner along our route home. I didn't want to spend any more time with her. Not like this. It could have been a good day—and maybe I'd wanted it to be—but she stopped being able to have fun on her own a long time before that day.

EIGHT

The girl stares ahead blankly, jaw loose and lids slack over her eyes. She filled her favorite glass with water and ice, sat in her favorite seat—the one we leave empty because it was hers—but she doesn't appear to know the significance of any of those things. She doesn't look like a girl who's home for the first time in over a year. She looks like a girl with barely enough energy to exist.

"Shel? It's me. It's Cara," I say.

She offers no response, no sign she even heard me.

"Is it really you?" I reach out, half expecting my hand to go straight through the figure sitting in front of me, but it catches on the fabric of her T-shirt, still cold from the air outside. She flinches away from my touch, registering my presence for the first time.

Shelby is here in front of me. She came back.

But something is wrong.

Her once chestnut hair hangs like bright, white curtains on either side of her face. It looks freshly dyed, with no sign of brown where roots would grow in after a few days. Even her eyebrows have lightened, adding to the ghostliness of her pale complexion.

"Do you know where you are?" I sit in the seat across from her, tempted to take her hands in mine.

She hugs her knees closer to her body as if reading my thoughts.

Her body goes rigid and her eyes, paler brown than I remember, lock on me for a second. "It was home."

Was.

I cringe.

"This is still your home."

She blinks a couple times, and the tension in her body dissipates again. She deflates before me, expression going dull again as she looks away from my eyes.

"Where have you been?" I ask.

If not for the way her hands clench into fists, I would've thought she hadn't heard me. I watch her carefully, noticing the way she pinches her eyes shut and grinds her teeth as though she's bracing for impact from something I can't see. She fights something, beats it down so she can't hear it anymore, then forces herself to look at me.

"Shelby. Answer me," I say. "Where have you been?"

"You wouldn't understand."

"Try me," I say.

Awkwardness thick as cement fills the distance between us. It suffocates me. A thousand questions fill my head like it might explode. Why did she leave? Why come back now?

"You can tell me what happened. I want to help you."

She looks away, fixing her gaze on the wall behind me again.

"I shouldn't have come back here. It's too dangerous," she whispers.

"It's safe here. We can protect you." Even if I can't, our parents can, the police can.

Shelby ignores the reassurance.

She sits so perfectly still in her chair, it unsettles me. Shelby didn't sit still before. Every waking moment had been spent tapping, twitching, fiddling with anything she could get a hold of. She couldn't be still. It was impossible.

This girl in front of me may wear the face of my sister, but I don't recognize the person behind it.

"Please. Tell me what happened. I promise I won't be angry with you."

"It's better if you don't know."

Dread creeps over me, ominous and overpowering. How can I help her if she won't let me? I need to call the police. I need my phone, but I left it in my room and I don't dare leave her here alone. She could disappear in the seconds it takes for me to retrieve it.

"You used to tell me everything. Why not now? Why won't you trust me?"

If she'd just open up, I could ask her why she didn't tell me she planned to leave, or if she even planned to leave at all. If she'd needed something, I could've helped. I could ask her for answers I filled in on my own, answers that left me angry.

"Because." Her eyes darken, a storm raging inside them. "I can't trust you anymore."

Her words land like a brick to my chest, and it takes a minute for me to catch my breath and speak again. "Of course you can."

"No. You'll just try convincing me I'm wrong and you know better, like you always used to. I don't need a lecture from you."

"What?" I try to make her look at me by inserting myself into her line of sight. "Why would you say that?"

"You gave me so much shit for spending money, or not caring enough at school, or wanting to quit working at the supermarket." Shelby's voice raises slightly. "You thought I was stupid for wanting to have fun instead of working all the time. You thought everything I did was wrong."

Her words freeze in the air just before they plunge into my heart, skewering the critical organ keeping me alive.

"Why would I tell you anything? I've been through enough without you reminding me how I've ruined my own life."

"I—"

I open my mouth to defend myself, but footsteps interrupt me from the direction of the living room where my parents sleep. Shelby stares down the hall to see who's coming. Does she remember that the shuffling of slippers belongs to Mom, while the padding of bare feet is Dad? If she did, she'd know she woke Dad.

"Well, Dad's up. Talk to him, then," I say. "All I wanted was to help you."

"You can't help. None of you can help." Her voice lowers again, barely audible now. "I came home to see you all one last time. I shouldn't have. It won't let me go."

I can't fight the urge to respond, to reassure her. "This isn't the last time you'll see us. You're home. Whatever happened, we'll get you through it."

"It's not that simple. I've done something unforgivable, and it followed me here."

NINE

Dad drops the cell phone he must've grabbed on the nightstand when he enters the kitchen and finds, not one, but both his daughters at the table. The glass face of the device shatters when the corner hits the floor, and the sound of it—sharp pieces cracking beneath the impact—makes the moment real. Dad ignores the damage as he rushes to Shelby and throws his arms around her in a hug.

"Liz, get in here," he calls to Mom.

Shelby squirms out of his grip in a way she never used to. She throws her elbows at him in a violent, jagged motion to keep him away. She looks like the embrace caused her pain, not just discomfort.

What happened to her?

Mom scuffles down the hallway, still groggy from sleep, and mutters incoherent words to Dad. I can't translate her tired slurs into words, but he does.

"She's back. Shelby's back."

I remain in my chair and watch the two of them process the return of their oldest daughter. Dad's eyes water at the edges and Mom's face turns a strawberry color like it does when she gets upset. They fawn over her like a newborn, like a puppy, instead of an eighteen-year-old girl.

Now that I get a chance to really look at her, she looks sick. Her face is gaunt, with sharp cheekbones where there hadn't been such dramatic angles before and eyes surrounded by a dark shadow that's more than just the smudged makeup. Her skin, already pale to begin with, has gone grayish and translucent. A pink T-shirt hangs too loose over her body, and the skinny jeans she wears sag around her thighs. She'd been thin when she left, but now it looks like she carved out organs just to drop their weight.

She shies away from my parents' touch the way she shied from mine. When Mom or Dad get too close, she winces like their presence burns.

I glance around the room, suddenly fixated on how she isn't dressed for the temperature. Her shirt carried a chill from outside when I touched it earlier.

"Where's your coat?" I ask her.

She ignores me.

I go to the mudroom to search for a jacket or sweatshirt, but find nothing. She came here with only the clothes she wears now. She should be frozen.

"You look so tired, Shel. Have you slept? How did you get home?" Mom says as I return to the kitchen.

"Hitchhiking." The right corner of Shelby's mouth twitches as the word passes her lips. A lie.

I don't call her out.

My parents' bodies go rigid at the thought of her in cars with strangers, of walking alongside the road with her thumb out. As if she hasn't been among strangers for the last year.

"You hitchhiked?" Dad breathes.

Shelby shrugs like it isn't a big deal.

As my parents attempt to get answers about where she's been and what she's been doing, I watch my sister get more and more uncomfortable. Her eyes dart back and forth like she wants to escape but can't decide whether the door or the window would be faster. Her lips go white as she presses them tightly together to keep her secrets in. The bones in her shoulders and elbows become visible beneath her thin skin as she curls up as small as she can to avoid being touched.

The words she said before Dad woke up linger with me. *I've done something unforgivable, and it followed me here.*

What does that mean?

A sour taste manifests in the back of my throat, and I imagine what brought my sister to this moment. Had she been imprisoned somewhere, starved of the food and attention she once craved? Or had she spent the whole year running from something she thought we couldn't forgive? What kind of misery made her look like this?

I wipe my sweaty palms on my sweatpants-clad thighs and try pushing the ideas away.

"We need to bring her to the hospital," Mom says in an attempt to pull herself back together. "They can help her."

When she goes to stuff her hands in pockets that don't exist on her flannel pajama bottoms, her face drops. The time of night, the fact that her daughter—her missing and presumed dead daughter—sits mere feet from where she stands... it all hits her at once.

"Shelby." Mom says my sister's name, testing it to see if it will crumble when it hits the air and take with it the illusion of a girl sitting at the table.

But my sister remains.

Shelby bristles at the mention of the hospital, and she

doesn't look invincible anymore. She looks like a cornered animal, eyes wide and afraid. It looks strange on her, the fear of not knowing what comes next. She clutches her hands so tight, they go dead white.

"I can't go to the hospital."

"You aren't in any trouble," Dad reassures her.

"No."

Shelby rises from her seat and makes for the door. Mom watches in horror as Shelby puts her hand on the doorknob and goes to leave, but Dad catches her before she gets outside.

"I'm not going to the hospital!" Shelby seethes.

Dad lifts her so her feet no longer touch the ground, and she kicks her legs and flails her arms in an attempt to break free.

"We need to make sure nobody hurt you," Dad says. "Liz, call the sheriff and tell them to meet us at the hospital."

Mom stands frozen in the kitchen, watching the scene unfold.

Shelby shrieks, still trying to get away from Dad.

I go to the landline on the wall and dial the number for the sheriff's office. A tired-sounding man answers, and I tell him Shelby came home and that we're taking her to the hospital. He says he'll send a couple deputies out in a half hour.

My heart pounds in my chest at the thought of doctors or police uncovering things Shelby lived through while she was gone. I don't want to learn about the last year of her life from someone else.

I thought my life couldn't change the way it did when Shelby disappeared, but her return has shaken everything up.

It all feels like the moments leading up to an accident. I see it coming, but it's too late to stop it. We can only brace ourselves and wait for the impact to tear us apart again.

"Shelby, is there anything you want to tell us before we get to the hospital?" Dad asks.

She says nothing, but tries again to wriggle free.

My sister didn't lie when it mattered, not when the truth was as serious as this. She lied to the school office to excuse our absences—they must have wondered why we always got sick together, really—and to our parents when we weren't where we were supposed to be. She'd lie to sneak out to parties on the weekends, and when we came back she'd have a whole story about the night we didn't have. She tried to lie when time she got caught changing someone's license plate motto from "10,000 Lakes" to "10,000 Dicks" using the label maker she "borrowed" from school.

She wouldn't lie about this, wouldn't keep dangerous secrets.

The air in the kitchen turns thick and no one speaks. I want to tell my parents what Shelby said, but I can't bring myself to do it. I want her to trust me again. I want to prove I can keep her secrets too. The reasons she thinks she can't trust me sting. All I wanted—all I *want*—is to help her, and I wish I'd known she resented me for it.

When Dad gets Shelby to settle down a bit, my parents change one at a time so the other can supervise her. Mom watches her vigilantly, prepared to do whatever it takes to keep her from going out the door and leaving again.

I get dressed without showering and dump last night's history book into my backpack with the others.

"You should stay home from school today," Mom says at the sight of my bag.

"No," I argue. I need this sense of normalcy while Shelby goes to the hospital. "I have a history test. Mel is expecting me."

"I'm sure your teacher will understand if you need to make it up later. Who is it? Mr. Clark?"

I nod, though I don't want to miss school. I don't want to spend the day in the hospital where I can't help. I'll only get in the way. Shelby won't talk if I'm around, and I want the doctors or police to figure out what's wrong so I can have my sister back. The version of her here is a fake, like only her body came back and not her soul.

"If things settle this afternoon, you can go to Mel's."

Blood peeks out from beneath the skin around my thumbnail. I've been picking it for longer than I've realized.

"I have responsibilities. She depends on me to be there."

Mom holds up a hand to end the conversation.

"Right now, your sister needs you. It's important you be there to support her." Dad switches into the voice he uses with his patients. It infuriates me, but I don't argue anymore. The four of us head to the car, and Dad sits in the back with Shelby, as if he thinks she might dive from the moving vehicle to escape going to the hospital.

TEN

After the doctors examine Shelby, they recommend she remain in the hospital for a couple days so they can keep an eye on her. She doesn't protest out loud, but the way her brow furrows suggests she wants to leave.

Mom and I sit in the two uncomfortable chairs in Shelby's room, while Dad stands with his arms crossed and talks to the nurses about what they've found. He walks the fine line between his role as a doctor himself and as the patient's parent, occasionally slipping into medical jargon he then has to explain to Mom before she panics again.

A nurse in toothpaste green scrubs replaces the now-empty bag of fluids hung about Shelby's bed.

"Can you tell me when you last had anything to eat?"

The question has been asked no less than a dozen times in the two hours we've been here, and my sister hasn't given an answer yet. Nobody needs it to know she hasn't eaten in a long time—long enough to wither down to skin and bones. The doctor had to order a special diet for her in addition to the fluids, but she refused the first meal.

"Aren't you hungry, Shel?" Mom asks.

Shelby doesn't even bother to shake her head, but she looks hungry. When the nurse set her first meal on a little table in front of her, Shelby's eyes widened. She stared at the food like a starved animal, but she didn't reach for the plastic spoon beside the bowl. All the muscles in her body went rigid, fighting a battle against the part of her that prevented her from eating.

In the end, she let the food go cold and ignored it until the nurse took it away.

We sit together for a while before the police come in. Mom thinks we should give Shelby one more chance to speak up before the deputies start asking their questions. Shelby doesn't say anything.

Instead, Shelby observes the deputies with skepticism. Her eyes narrow to daggers as the cops stand beside her bed in what appears to be their best attempt at not intimidating her.

"I'm Deputy Mendes," a tan-skinned woman with dark curls says. "This is Deputy Rawson."

Beside Deputy Mendes, a white man with ruddy cheeks reaches out to shake Shelby's hand. Shelby keeps hers folded in her lap, disinterested in being polite.

"We're going to ask you a few questions, and appreciate it if you'll answer us honestly so we can understand where you've been," Deputy Mendes says.

A flicker of amusement crosses Shelby's expression.

The deputies either don't see it or don't recognize it, because they flip open their notebooks and get to work as if they don't already know Shelby has no plans of saying anything to either of them.

She said she came home to see us all one last time, and I wonder what she could have meant. Is she dying? Does she plan to disappear again? Is someone after her? I can't bear the thought of losing her a second time. Now that she's here, I allow myself to hope life can go back to normal again. Shelby and I will pick up where we left off, and I will forgive her for the things she said before she vanished.

An hour passes before the deputies change their tactic. Deputy Rawson asks me and my parents who found Shelby, then, when he finds out it was me, asks me to come talk with him outside the room.

I pick at my fingernails once we settle in the quiet corner of the mostly empty waiting room. He rifles through his notepad until he finds the page where he left off with his notes, not that he'd been given much to take down.

"How are you doing with all of this?" Rawson asks in a voice more suited to broken people than to me.

"I'm tired, and... my sister hates me." It hurts to say it out loud, but it hurts more to think of the things she said to me.

"What makes you say that?"

I repeat the things Shelby said earlier about how she doesn't trust me and doesn't want my help. I'd spent so many nights wondering if I'd played a part in her leaving. Maybe if I hadn't made her feel bad about her choices, would she have stayed?

Rawson jots everything I say down in messy handwriting on his notepad.

"I don't know what to do. I want to help her, but I don't know how."

He doesn't try telling me how to handle this. "It will take time," he says. "Your sister went through something traumatic while she was missing, and she will tell us when she's ready."

She already told me something. What if it was a test?

What if she gave me those small pieces of information to see if I really could be trusted?

"Did her behavior strike you as unusual when you found her?" Rawson asks.

"She seems... I don't know. Tired? Her whole personality is gone, or something. The only time she seemed right, she was angry with me."

His pen scratches against the paper some more, and I keep talking.

"I couldn't sleep, so I went into the kitchen to get a glass of water and she was just... there. At the table." Exhausted, the accent I hate slips out. Some of the words get drawn out with long vowels, the way people talk when they're making a joke of the Midwest. The way people who have only seen *Fargo* or interviews of Packers fans think we talk.

"Why couldn't you sleep? Did something wake you?"

"My cat. Something in the woods freaked her out, and she was acting strange. It kept me up."

He clicks the end of the pen a couple times before he asks his next question.

"Did you see what it was? A car pulling in the driveway, maybe? Headlights coming in through the window? Those things would be enough to wake me up."

"No, it wasn't that. My dad usually comes home from work in the middle of the night, so Charlie—uh, Charlie's my cat—is a master at sleeping through that stuff. It was definitely..." I pause, choosing my words carefully. "... an animal Charlie saw."

"Are you sure?"

"Yes."

I realize I have no idea how Shelby got to the house in the middle of the night, dressed in summer clothes. She must have gotten a ride. She couldn't have walked to the house dressed like that. There's no way.

Deputy Rawson might be able to figure it out, but I can't keep what I know from him. He could track down whoever brought her home. It might send him in the direction of the truth.

"She's really messed up. She won't make eye contact. She hardly moves. I don't understand." I have to tell him what she said. Even if it means she doesn't trust me with anything else, fine. She gave me a few words, little shreds of information that don't mean much to me but might mean something to the police. "She told me… " I pause, tell myself this will help her. Maybe she'll forget she told me, and when the deputy inevitably asks her about it, she won't trace it back to me. I doubt I'll be so lucky.

"What did she tell you?"

"She said she came home to see us one last time, like she plans on something happening to her. And she said she did something bad that followed her here. I don't know. I don't know how she got here, or what she meant."

Three of my nails sting from where I picked away the skin, and blood wells up at the edge of each.

"She lied. She told my parents she hitchhiked home."

"This is very helpful, Cara. Thank you."

"You're welcome. Please, figure out what happened to her. She doesn't deserve this."

He nods, somber. "Sometimes, people handle complicated things by retreating inward. She could still be processing everything that happened, and it's all she can do to work through it. She won't recover overnight, but what matters is she's here now." Deputy Rawson sounds like an optimist to me. He makes me tired.

ELEVEN

Parker's Camry idled in the fire lane in front of Nice-N-Spice when Shelby and I walked out in our matching uniforms. His older sister had come through another line and bought a bunch of cheap beer, so I figured Shelby wouldn't be coming home with me. Still, I hoped she would skip the party tonight.

"I'm going to Parker's tonight," she said.

"Oh. I thought we were going to watch *Captain America...* " I tried not to sound too disappointed, but the DVD from the Redbox in front of the store weighed heavy in my bag beside a package of Raisinets. Shelby liked those best.

"Next weekend, okay?"

I started to tell her I'd already gotten the movie for tonight, but it wouldn't have mattered. She'd do what she wanted. Hours before, she'd wanted to have movie night together like old times, but that was before she found something better to do.

"Yeah." I said.

"Great!" She tossed her keys at me, though I wasn't ready and they landed on the cement sidewalk in front of me. *Asshole*, I thought as I scooped them up.

My sister climbed into the backseat of the Camry and Parker sped off, leaving me in a cloud of exhaust.

"Okay, then," I said to no one. "I'll go watch *Captain America* by myself."

I walked to where Shelby had parked the truck that morning and climbed in. I hated driving it at night, but she left me no choice. Something on the dashboard lit up when I started the engine—no gas. If I wanted to be a jerk, I could've driven home on fumes and left her to figure out the fifteen-minute drive to the nearest station, but I didn't. Filling up at the painfully slow analog pump gave me time to prepare to lie to Mom again. As pissed as I was, Shelby and I had an unspoken rule that sisters kept one another's secrets, even if one of them had nothing worth telling.

TWELVE

Rawson runs out of questions for me, so I excuse myself to the bathroom and splash cold water on my face. A fan in the center of the ceiling rattles with age and drowns out my thoughts for a while.

I didn't expect it to be like this. I thought, if Shelby came home, the worst would be over. All the times I imagined her return, I imagined her saying she's embarked on a great adventure. I pictured her well fed, with sunkissed skin from whatever beach town she called home for a while. All my scenarios had her healthy, because I couldn't imagine her doing anything she didn't choose herself. I didn't want to consider a possibility where she didn't go on purpose.

But she came back broken and sick, and I don't know what to do now.

I can't deal with this.

I finally stopped looking for her. Finally kicked my addiction to driving back roads and searching for a lost girl roaming the streets. When I found nothing, I took more hours at the supermarket and tried to fill every last second in the day.

Now, with work and school and volunteering with Mel's fosters, I barely have time to sleep. There is no time to add anything else, but this is my sister. I have to help her, even if she's pissed at me. Even if she hates me.

I splash more water on my face, then return to my sister's room. The deputies stand side by side with their notepads ready. Mom leans against Dad, like she's desperate for warmth or support or both. Shelby's eyes smolder in their sockets.

"Sisters keep one another's secrets," she says in a low growl.

I flinch at her words.

Instinct makes me open my mouth to tell her I had to, to try to appease her. I don't want her to be mad at me.

Fuck it.

"You don't get to have secrets right now." A spark of adrenaline moves through my body. "You have to tell us what happened so we can help you."

My sister's brow furrows and she balls her fists around the blanket on either side of her legs. "You can't help me."

"The police can. This is their job."

"No. They'll die too. People will die if you don't let me go." She reaches for the IV in her arm, but Dad stops her from tearing it out.

"Don't. You'll hurt yourself," he says.

She looks up at him, eyes glazed over from exhaustion. "Nothing hurts me anymore." Her voice transforms to something soft, fragile, like the fight in her that keeps her on edge has faded for a moment.

"We understand you're afraid and have been through a lot, but I assure you we can protect you," Deputy Mendes says.

"You couldn't protect Parker or Emily."

I swallow hard, trying not to think about her friends. Parker died—was killed—ten days before Shelby disappeared. I don't ask how she knows about Emily, whose body was found in the woods two months after. People in town talked about whether Shelby would turn up next.

"Those were animal attacks due to your friends being out in the woods in the winter. Animals can't find much to eat during that time of year. They get desperate." Mendes recites the words like a practiced line. "Were you out in the woods with them?"

Shelby releases her hold on the blanket beside her, and drags one of her nails along the metal railing on her bed. "No."

The air thickens in my lungs. Deep in the pit of my stomach, something screams out that what Shelby is saying is wrong or incomplete. I want there to be more to the story, to her answer.

"Did you know there's a monster in the woods?" Shelby says, still dragging her nail along the metal. "It hurts people, and I've done terrible things so it won't hurt me too."

Mom looks over at Dad, malignant worry in her eyes. My throat has been filled with cement. Even the police seem to have lost their words.

We all wait in silence, like maybe Shelby will keep talking without us reminding her. She doesn't.

"You can tell us what you did. Whatever it was, it wasn't your fault," Dad says.

"We won't be upset with you, Shel. I promise. We can't..."

We can't lose you again.

But Mom can't finish the sentence.

THIRTEEN

Once the police leave—or, really once they give up—Mom agrees to take me home so I can get the truck and go to Mel's. The entire ride home, I dwell on everything Shelby said about monsters and bad things done to escape them.

The police think she's delirious or experiencing withdrawal from something—though I don't think they meant for me to hear. They don't think it's an actual monster. They think it's the human kind, the type of person we elevate to nightmare status because of the things they've done.

The thought makes me shiver.

Mom waits in the doorway while I grab my things, as if she's nervous about me being in the house alone. I almost tell her she doesn't need to, that I've been in this place alone so many times since Shelby left, that this house isn't what took her away, but I don't. The sound of her footsteps in the kitchen comforts me.

In my room, I pick up my phone for the first time all day. An annoying red circle above the messages app shows me I have twenty-eight texts. I don't think I even know twenty-eight people.

Word has already gotten out about Shelby's return, and most of the messages are from kids at school asking how she is. I delete all but two of them. The first I keep is from Mel, asking if I want the night off. I respond, insisting it will be good for me to fall into my normal routine. Then, I move on to the other text.

A message from Marie came somewhere in the middle of all the messages I don't care about. I still have her contact in my phone, and it stands out against the numbers I don't recognize.

I heard Shelby's back. I'm here if you need someone to talk to.

I pinch my eyes shut against the prickling feeling Marie's text gives me. It would be so easy to take her up on her offer, and she must know it. She must think I have no one to talk to.

I test out a few words to see if I have anything to say in response, but everything feels weird. Forced. Instead, I clear out the text bubble and delete the message like the rest of them.

It leaves behind a dangerous feeling of nostalgia—or maybe only a reminder of the empty space she left behind. Marie had always been the one to text when things went wrong. Somehow, she always knew I had a rough day at work or got a bad grade on a school assignment. She said she could tell by the tone of my texts, could tell without seeing my face or hearing my voice.

Even separated by two towns, she never felt distant. Sometimes, I forget I cut her out. Sometimes she still feels close, but believing that would be a mistake. She has Cassandra now.

I pocket the phone, say goodbye to Mom, and get into the truck, alone. I travel down roads obscured by the coming dusk. A cold as deep as my bones settles in. I'm so tired of the winter. So goddamn tired of warmth being just out of reach.

The space between trees beckons me with whispers planted directly in my head. One slip of my hands and it could pull me in with a violent crash against the bodies of thick elms and spruces. The roots would grow up and around, trapping me in the cab of this Dodge for the rest of eternity. They would take me, sap the nutrients from my body until, one day, I become part of the forest and only my bones remain.

People have long said the woods are their own being, with wants and needs like anything else. The tree line marks the boundary between safety and their territory. If I cross it, the forest will devour me like it did my sister before it spat her out broken.

Hope the dog greets me with a single, polite lick on my hand when I slip through Mel's front door and yank my boots off. I scratch the dog beneath her chin for a minute before she returns to Mel's side.

"How's Shelby?" Mel gets straight to business. "How're your parents? How are you?"

"We're okay, all things considered. Shelby though... she's... I don't know."

Mel nods, somehow understanding.

I fill Mel in on the events of the morning, on all the things Shelby said. Even though I've turned them over in my head dozens of times now, saying them aloud makes them more solid. When I finish, I take a long breath and hold it in my lungs for a while. "This isn't what I expected."

"It'll take time for her to open up again," Mel says. "Be patient. You've been through a lot too, and need to be kind to yourself while you figure out how to process this."

I sigh, go to the fridge and take two cans of pop from the shelf. "I don't know how to process it. She's giving me nothing to process."

Mel cracks her pop open, then takes a long drink. I take small sips of mine. The sugar tastes too sweet, and I swear the caffeine hits my brain like a jolt of electricity.

"Information will come when she's ready. Just be there for her like you always were. She needs her sister."

I frown into the can of pop. Shelby always needed me. She'd lean on me when she couldn't bear to be around the people at school, but couldn't be alone either. And I was always there for her, always set aside my own life to help bear the weight of hers.

"What if I don't want to wait?" I say. I have a bad idea, one I'd hate more if I weren't so desperate. It's been lingering in the back of my mind for hours now, ever since Shelby uttered the word *monster*. "What if there were someone with a history of tracking things that I could ask for help?"

Mel gapes. She knows exactly who I mean. "His family tracks, I don't know, coyotes. Not criminals."

"Sure. But he's obsessed with monsters. He'll help if I tell him what Shelby said."

"Cara... " Mel frowns at my idea. I do too. But nobody else in this town will go into those woods looking for a murderer or a kidnapper or whatever. "This isn't good. Let the police handle this."

"I'll ask him. If he doesn't want to, he doesn't have to. No big deal."

If I know Lucas the way I think I do, he'll jump at the idea to search for Shelby's monster. It doesn't matter that I don't think she's telling the truth. All that matters is I'm doing something about it.

FOURTEEN

The house greeted me with noise. Shelby sang off-key along with the newish Panic! At The Disco album, which blared from the speakers of a partially blown-out iPhone dock. The whirring of a hand mixer I thought had broken years ago hums, barely audible, beneath the music.

Shelby did that thing she always does where she starts baking before realizing she's missing a key ingredient. Cocoa powder. Like, it would be impossible to finish the brownies she'd started without it, and I wasn't about to let her throw the pale batter away. So I went to the store for her and bought some, which I set on the counter beside the bowl.

"Store brand?" Shelby said over the music.

She inspected the metal canister as if it contained dirt instead of cocoa.

"It was a dollar cheaper. It'll do," I said.

Shelby measured out the right amount of cocoa and

mixed it into the batter then poured it into a pan and stuck it in the oven. Just before she closed the oven door, she stood there and took in the heat coming from within. A soft smile spread across her face, and she closed her eyes for a second. She basked in the rare moment of comfort before letting the door slam shut.

I hadn't seen her in a mood like this in a long time. So long, I wasn't quite sure when the last time was that she was happy, and without the help of alcohol.

"Okay, so I think I figured it out." She made the declaration as she licked brownie batter off her fingers. "Costa Rica."

I blinked at her.

"Costa Rica, Cara. That's where we'll go."

The conversation—one we'd had dozens of times—flooded in all at once. We often fantasized about where we'd live when we finally left Wolf Hill. We always wanted somewhere warm, but sometimes we imagined ourselves in Australia, other times, a tiny island in the Pacific. This time, after months of deliberation since our last talk, Shelby had landed on Costa Rica.

"You can bring Marie, if she wants to come, and we can all live in the jungle with the little monkeys."

Though the brownies had only been in for a few minutes, Shelby opened the oven again. Said she had to make sure they looked right.

I balled up the receipt from the supermarket and tossed it into the trash, then took my place at the sink where dishes sat in a heap. Shelby had used every measuring cup, every utensil, every bowl in the house. They all sat in a few inches of brownie batter dyed water that had grown tepid.

"What about Parker?" I asked. "Wouldn't you want him to come?"

Shelby shut the oven again, a hot breeze brushing against my exposed forearms.

"I don't know."

I created a new pile of dishes, clean ones, to one side of the sink. Shelby didn't take the hint to dry them.

"What do you mean you don't know? You've been together for six months," I said.

Shelby hadn't been dating Parker as long as I'd been with Marie, but six months still felt like a big deal. It was a big deal for Shelby, who went through boys like fire through paper. Parker, so far, had lasted the longest.

My sister drummed on the counter with her fingers. Restlessness seemed to creep in with the mention of her boyfriend. She seemed on the verge of losing hold on her good mood, and I wanted to preserve it. Not as bad as I wanted to know why she was being weird about Parker, though.

"I don't know how long he'll be around," Shelby said. "He's fun, but I just don't feel it anymore. You know?"

"No. I really don't know. Tell me."

I turned around and leaned against the sink. A thin line of water along the edge seeped into the fabric of my shirt and sent a chill through my body. Shelby sat on the ground, legs crossed, and looked in on the brownies as they baked.

"It's just... it gets old being with someone who thinks they need to babysit you. He has these parties, and they're great, but he spends half his time following me around and telling me not to drink too much."

"Oh."

"It's like he thinks I can't take care of myself, and I don't know why everyone seems to think that about me." Her eyes go glassy as she talks, and, though my sister sits mere feet from me, her mind has gone somewhere else for now.

FIFTEEN

Mom keeps me home from school one more day, and, though I fight her on it, I guess I'm glad to have a little more time before having to face kids at school and their questions. Besides, it gives me a chance to think about how to approach Lucas without scaring him away. Will he even help me? When the idea first struck, it seemed like a sure shot. I'd say, "Hey Lucas! Shelby said a monster took her," and he'd be all "okay let's go find it." No questions asked.

But now, the more that I think about it, the more I worry he'll be skeptical of me coming to him with this. He knows I don't believe in the things he does. He knows I punched him for suggesting the very thing I plan on telling him tomorrow. Ugh. I really shouldn't have done that... it didn't even feel good at the time.

By the time I get to school on Friday, I still don't have a solid grasp on what to do. I'll take a page out of Shelby's book and figure it out as I go, as uncharacteristic as that approach may be.

As expected, people come at me from all angles to

bombard me with comments about how they never gave up on finding her—as if *I* did? Okay.—and questions about what she said happened while she was gone. None of it is their business, so I duck away from them and hurry to class. Hopefully, once people realize I won't talk, they'll leave me alone.

"Miss Hughes," my teacher, Mr. Marshall, begins. I assume he means to ask some of the same questions everyone else has, though I'd be surprised if he did that in front of the whole class. "Glad to have you back. I hope you and your family are doing okay."

A sigh of relief escapes my lungs when he doesn't press the matter further. The whole day will be full of people demanding information.

The kid behind me taps me on the shoulder, and I turn to see what they want. One of the football kids looks at me, bored out of his mind, and offers me a hot pink note card that's been folded at least four times.

My nerves fray for a moment at the possibility of the note being about Shelby. People are bolder in what they'll say when they think they're anonymous, and Wolf County has no shortage of people who will say horrible things for attention.

"Lucas wanted me to pass this," he says in a quiet baritone.

I take the note, then wait for Mr. Marshall to turn to the whiteboard before I slip the note beneath my desk and unfold it. The handwriting is neat, the question blunt. I read it twice, three times.

She didn't tell you anything, did she?

He doesn't know I need him yet, so the note pisses me off. What makes him think I want to talk to him now? The fact that I do is not important.

Actually, I need to talk to you about something... B lunch. Library.

I pass the note back via the kid between us, then let regret settle in. Maybe Mel is right. Maybe this is a bad idea. Maybe I shouldn't take advantage of Lucas's weird obsession with the supernatural. I don't have the energy to listen to his endless conspiracy theories about hidden monsters and government cover-ups, but that's what I'm getting myself into.

Every so often, Mr. Marshall looks my way. He might have noticed I've stopped paying attention, or maybe he wants to see if I've collapsed under the weight of worry. It wouldn't be unreasonable for him to think stress has consumed me, not with the way I tear at the skin on my fingertips as I await the note's return.

It lands with the whisper of paper against the surface of the desk. It seems so loud at first that I expect everyone to turn toward the sound, but no one does.

See you then.

I stuff the note in my bag and focus on whatever Mr. Marshall is talking about. The content of his lecture doesn't stick, and my mind wanders back to the place it's been for days now.

Whatever it is Lucas's family does—whether they hunt nuisance animals or are bounty hunters—it might not be enough. He might not know what to do, or how to help. He might not want to. I don't think I'd blame him.

But also, part of me hopes he is the right person to ask, that this won't be a waste of time.

"Mr. Powell," Mr. Marshall interjects, "would you like to share your obviously urgent thoughts with the class?"

Everyone, including me, turns to look at Lucas, who has another index card folded in one raised hand like he was about to throw it. His eyebrows rise in embarrassment about being caught, and he lowers the note.

"No, thank you," Lucas says.

"Then I'd appreciate it if you stopped throwing notes at other students. You'll have plenty of time outside of class to talk with your friends."

Mr. Marshall looks at me with a mix of disappointment and sympathy in his eyes. He must assume Lucas has been hassling me all class. It wouldn't be out of character for him.

After a year of it, I've grown sick of people's sympathy. The way people let their features soften into a more approachable expression. How their words dull on the corners so they won't hurt as much when they land. It gets old being treated like something fragile when you've spent so long teaching yourself to be strong. Though, now that Shelby's back, I'm not sure I'm strong enough.

SIXTEEN

My stomach growls as I sit in the front corner of the library waiting, impatiently, for Lucas. He's late. B lunch started exactly seventeen minutes ago, and, if I'd known I had that kind of time, I'd have gotten something to eat. Everyone else in the library must hear the sounds of my hunger, so I clutch my stomach to drown out the gurgling.

This was a bad idea. He's not coming.

Maybe he realized he doesn't want to help, since I've been such an asshole to him for the last year.

I open the paperback I need to read for class and force my eyes to focus. Too bad I didn't have breakfast either. A little sustenance might make my vision clear enough to see what the pages say.

"No food in the library," says the librarian in a voice that contradicts the other rule in his kingdom: be quiet. Even if he'd said it at a reasonable volume, I'd still be curious who dares bring food past these doors.

The offender stands between the metal scanners inside the door with a pizza from the gas station next to the school, and a backpack slung over the opposite shoulder. No coat, just a hoodie. A boy living on the edge.

"Cara, let's study somewhere else." Lucas defies the librarian one last time by calling over to me.

I choose to be amicable first because I asked for his help, and second because he has pizza.

"I thought you'd be hungry," he says. "Didn't think it would take forty minutes for them to make a veggie pizza though. Sorry."

Some of my annoyance fizzles from both the peace offering and the apology. "It's fine" is the closest thing to kindness I have to offer.

"We could eat in the hall, I guess." He looks around for somewhere to sit, but it's a risk.

"Nah. We'll eat in my truck. Less chance of people eavesdropping."

He gives me a questioning look.

"They don't need to be involved. I asked you for help, not the entire school."

Lucas seems fine with my reasoning, and walks beside me out to the parking lot where I left the truck somewhere in a sea of beat-up pickups and shiny base-model sedans. I unlock his side first for the sake of the pizza, then climb behind the wheel. The engine grumbles when I turn the key in the ignition, hoping the heat will work today. Then I reach for a slice of pizza.

"So," Lucas says through a mouthful of food, "what did you want to talk about?"

I take a bite of my slice of pizza to buy myself time before I say something I can't take back. Once I put this in motion, that's it.

The pizza eases the hunger, and, in turn, the nervousness stabbing at my stomach. It's the perfect balance of greasy and cheesy, with a mix of vegetables scattered on top to pass as healthy. I should thank him. I don't.

"Well?" he says through another mouthful of food.

"I'll get to it. It's just... hard to get my head around."

Lucas tosses his crust back into the box and takes another slice. I chew the cheese off the bones of mine, not one to waste food, and try and get a hold of my thoughts.

The claw marks on the side of the door seem to vibrate and remind me how wrong they are. They nag at me to consider the possibility of having been made by a beast other than a bear, but I won't. Despite what Shelby said, I cling to my reasonable explanations. I will always cling to them.

"She said there's a monster in the woods." I start with the simplest of phrases. "And she doesn't think the police can help protect her."

"What kind of monster?" he asks, curious like I expected.

"She didn't say. But she did say she had to do bad things so it wouldn't kill her. I don't know what she means, but since she said it was a monster, I thought you could help."

"Do you believe her?" A smug grin spreads across his face, and I glare at him. He shouldn't be satisfied.

"I... yes. I do." Every fiber of my being resists as I hold back my instincts and lie. "I trust my sister."

The grin on his face fades, and his expression turns thoughtful. "So you want my help hunting it."

"Everyone says your family hunts, and not just deer. The rumors make it seem like you have the right skills to figure this out." I hate myself. The words make it seem like Lucas works alongside Liam Neeson as an undercover agent. It dignifies his absurd conspiracy theories.

"What skills do you think I have?" he asks.

"I don't know. Your family hunts coyotes and things when they cause trouble at the farms. Right? Something like that?"

He laughs. No, he bellows. "Not quite," he says.

"Well, then tell me whether you can help me or not so I don't waste any more of my time," I snap. Honestly, I'll be kind of pissed if he can't even track a fox.

"If it's a monster you're after, a monster I will hunt."

I roll my eyes. "How? How exactly are you qualified for this? Don't you have an aunt or something with all the family secrets I can talk to instead?"

The talk of ridiculous, made-up creatures doesn't come. Maybe he's a bounty hunter or some kind of assassin in the mob. Minnesota must have a mob, right?

"No. It's just me and my mom now, and she can't hunt in her condition." His tone darkens. "I can help you, but you have to swear you won't tell anyone about this."

"About what?" I feel almost bad about playing dumb and leading him on. He should know I don't think Shelby's been held captive by a monster for a year. He has to know that.

Maybe he doesn't want to believe it.

"Cara, the Powell name has been passed down through generations of specialized hunters. Our directive has been protected from civilians for just as long, and I won't be the one who lets that secret get out. We have our clients sign a contract that says, if you tell anyone not included in the agreement about the nature of our work, you will be dealt with accordingly."

He sounds serious. Too serious. This isn't real, but I play along.

"I'll sign your contract." It won't be hard not to talk

about his work, because it's made-up. He's delusional. This is not a good idea.

Yet, something in my gut tells me to keep going. Desperation, maybe? Something in the rumors about the Powells must be rooted in truth.

"I'll do some research to make sure this is something I can help with, then I'll bring you the terms of our arrangement."

"Okay."

He puts his last crust in the box with the others, and takes a pen and leather notebook out from his backpack. "Tell me everything you can about your sister."

I tell him how her distant, empty eyes avoid locking their gaze with anyone else, about the way all the color in her has drained away. He knew her before—*everyone* knew her before—and his lips tighten with every word I say. This version of Shelby misaligns with the girl he knew. The one who came back is an off-brand imitation. Good enough if you never cared to begin with, but clearly an imposter if you look close enough.

"There's not much to go off here," he begins. "It'll take me a couple days to go through the database and come back with some ideas. If anything comes up, text me."

He tears a page from the notebook, blank except for his phone number, and hands it to me. Then, he climbs out of the truck and leaves me there with the remains of our pizza and a jagged sense of disbelief in my head.

What am I getting myself into?

SEVENTEEN

The Saturday morning rush keeps me distracted for most of the first half of my shift. Our lines back up into the aisles and people start getting frustrated over everything. Order gives way to anarchy with the first customer to demand a manager over the most asinine inconvenience, and I welcome the chaos. Angry people don't make small talk. If anything, they offer clipped answers to my usual questions like *did you find everything you needed today?*

The last thing I want is small-town small talk, because I know everyone's heard about Shelby. That means they've already heard the rumors people like to twist in a real-life game of telephone.

Eventually, the rush dies down as the hordes spill into the parking lot and disperse. Then I handle only a trickle of customers and make every attempt to stay busy. I almost ask Anna if she'll send me out to get carts, though I know she won't. She rarely sends me out in the cold to retrieve them from the corrals and, more often than not, from the snowbanks and dividers where people abandon them. Those in her good favor don't get cart duty.

"You know, Cara," Anna begins, approaching the end of my lane and refilling the plastic bags. I brace myself. "The nominees for the internship are finally in."

My chest clenches. I've been waiting for this for an eternity. The interview I had in June feels impossibly far behind me now.

What if I didn't get in?

I find a smile on Anna's face. It looks wrong on her. Sweat slicks my palms, and I dry them on my jeans. I want to know, but the fear of asking Anna whether I got in prevents me from speaking. The suspense kills me.

I've been holding on to the possibility of getting into this program since I first heard of it. Over time, it's become the only way I see myself getting a two-year degree, of moving up in the world and getting ahead. I'd be kidding myself if I thought I could afford school otherwise. I won't take the route my parents did, the one that left them weighed down by debt and at the mercy of the Department of Education.

"Don't you want to know?" Anna looks at me like a cat looks at a mouse. She'd eat me alive if given the chance, but not before having her fun. This is a game to her.

I want to remind her the store could benefit from me going to St. Cloud for the summer. *She* could benefit from having one of her employees get noticed. Like everything else, Wolf Hill left its mark on this store. The town drags the outdated building down with it as people leave, abandoning the hopelessness of here for the promise of there.

But if I got in, maybe corporate would fix the store up a bit. Maybe we'd get the new dry-fit polos they have in

Riverside. I don't know. Something would have to change. I'd make it change.

"Congratulations, Cara. You're in."

My muscles relax, lungs pull in a new breath, but nothing else happens. I'd expected the store to get brighter, cleaner, or for Anna to transform into someone more pleasant to work for. At the very least, my shirt would get less yellow.

But nothing changes, because in the back of my mind I know I can't celebrate right now.

"Thank you," I say.

Unspoken words hang in the air like Anna has more planned for this conversation. Like she didn't come over here only for the sake of telling me about the internship, but really showed up to talk about Shelby. She can't resist.

"So..." She puts both hands at the end of the lane, nudging my produce basket out of place. "What's all the stuff I've been hearing about Shelby?"

I hate being right.

"Like what? She's back, but that's all we know right now."

"People say she was kidnapped and the guy's coming for her now. Has she said anything about him? What if he comes for you?" Anna speaks in a fake whisper, and a customer two lanes over cranes her head to eavesdrop.

"People watch too much TV," I say.

Anna pouts, like actually puts her bottom lip forward like a spoiled child. She wanted me to give her something to cling to. A piece of exclusive information she should spin into a juicy story for the next person she reels in with her gossip. I can't even get out of the conversation. I'm a hostage in this spot until she sends me on break or decides I'm not worth the effort.

"Can you believe she came back after a year? You know, they say after the first forty-eight hours, the likelihood of finding someone alive is next to nothing. But she just walked back home. It's a great story."

"Yeah, totally." I pick at a piece of tape stuck to the bottom of the register's screen.

"Do you think she knows people think she killed her boyfriend?"

The question sends anger through me, sharp and hot, and I grit my teeth against the urge to snap. I can't snap. I fold my fingers on the counters so tight, the skin goes dead white and my heart races.

"Parker died in an animal attack," I say.

"Shelby's a smart girl. Smart enough to kill him and toss him in the woods for the wolves."

I've heard this theory so many times, I thought I'd gotten used to it. Even the police suggested it once or twice, but ruled it out when a second victim of the same type of attack turned up, then a third. We had an animal problem, and I was more willing to believe Shelby had fallen victim to it than I was to believe she pulled together some mastermind scheme to kill her friends and three other random people.

"That isn't what happened, and you know it."

"Oh, Cara, you need to lighten up. Go take your break, okay?"

I flip the switch on my register and disappear into the breakroom before Anna has the chance to change her mind. I can't let her see my face, flushed hot from holding back frustration at her for talking about my sister like our lives were an episode of some cheap crime drama. I can't even stand up for Shelby, because I can't have Anna turning on me if I say the wrong thing. I have to stay quiet and ignore. That's part of this job, especially now. She's fired people for less, and now I know I got the internship. I can't lose this.

EIGHTEEN

S helby sat at her usual spot at the table when I came into the house. She looked pissed off or bored as she stared at the black screen of her phone, but I couldn't decide which.

"Shouldn't you be at Parker's party?" I asked.

"His dad's got the cabin tonight. Bear season."

"Um. Did he tell you that?" Shit. Not again. Parker didn't seem like the type to lie.

Her mouth formed a thin line, and she held her phone out to me. It was open to a text thread with Parker.

Shelby: *What time should I meet you later?*

Parker: *Party's canceled. Dad's using the cabin.*

Parker: *He and my uncle went hunting. They want a bear.*

Shelby: *Wanna go to Riverside and see a movie?*

Parker: *Can't. Hunting with dad.*

Shelby: *Oh...*

Beneath the messages, Shelby had typed something

else. *I didn't think you liked hunting???* but hadn't sent it. The last message was read hours ago.

"I should have seen this coming," she said as she took back the phone. "He's such an asshole."

I pulled out the chair across from her, though I had homework to do. The work would have to wait. I needed to talk Shelby down from the mood she was about to fall into, or she'd find her own way of dealing with it. Probably with the bottle of Canadian whiskey stashed in her closet.

"Are things okay with you two?" I asked.

"Do they seem okay to you?" she snapped.

I poked again, knowing I'd get her wrath. "Well, what's going on?"

She crossed her arms tight over her chest and looked out the window beside the table. If a look could transport a person somewhere far away, she'd have been gone.

"You saw the texts. He lied to me."

"Why?"

"He thinks I'm a drunk or something. He thinks I don't know when to stop."

"Do you know when to stop?"

Shelby glared at me, like my question was an instant betrayal. "I'm not stupid, Cara."

There were so many things I could have said. I could've told her that alcoholism has nothing to do with being stupid or smart, that it's a disease like the depression she took pills for every day. Could've reminded her about Parker's mom's time in rehab. But she wouldn't have heard those things. She couldn't. Not when she was angry.

I rose from my seat, and Shelby pulled her phone closer to herself possessively. She unlocked the screen and began typing again.

"He'll be sorry," she muttered.

"Don't text him right now, Shel."

Her head snapped up and she looked at me with burning eyes. "Don't do that. Don't tell me what to do."

I held my hands up and took a step back. She returned to furiously typing on her phone, and I considered for a second trying to take the device away from her.

Instead, I took her keys with me to my room and left her at the table.

NINETEEN

Fat snowflakes hit my windshield and make it impossible to see the road. My headlights reflect off them and create a blinding sheet of white, forcing me to slow to a crawl if I want to stay out of the ditch. Heavy bags of sand slide around in the back of the truck, weighing down the bed so I won't fishtail up the hills. Still, every now and then, a jolt of panic seizes my heart when I hit a patch of ice. I hold the wheel with both hands and lean forward in my seat, shoulders tense, as if being slightly closer will make my vision any better.

As much as I hate the cold, I don't mind the snow—though driving in it sucks. At the very least, it looks pretty when it blankets the town. It makes everything look newer, cleaner. In the hours after a fresh snow, this town looks a little less sad.

Ahead, the bright red lights of the back of a car catch my attention. The sight of it on the side of the road makes my breath hitch in my throat. The light on the inside glows, and the driver's side door gapes open. When I pull over behind it, I find snow collecting on the seats. Nobody's inside.

I could probably pull them out of the ditch, if they needed. I think. Though, I have to find the driver first.

When my boots hit the ground, snow reaches midway up my calves. Slush sneaks through my jeans and nips at the skin on my legs as I trudge through the snow to the open door of the car. With the flashlight on my cell phone, I look around.

Guess I won't be pulling the car out. The front end of the otherwise spotless, silver Jetta is crushed against a tree, hood crumpled like aluminum foil. Airbags lay deflated against the dashboard and steering wheel. The keys still hang from the ignition and choppy music plays from the radio, haunting the scene with white noise.

Thin streams of liquid trail down the bag that caught the driver who no longer occupies their seat.

My pulse quickens at the sight of the blood.

"Hello?" I call out. "Is anyone here? Do you need help?"

My heart slams against my ribs as the staticky silence engulfs me.

I should call the police and let them handle this, but the goddamn trees block any chance I have at calling anyone.

Someone could be hurt. They could have wandered into the forest, disoriented and afraid. I could help them.

But there's no proof anyone walked into the forest. The missing driver could've walked down the road, unfamiliar with the distance between everything here, in hopes of finding help.

I take a step away from the trees.

The darkness between them calls to me. It tells me to come be a hero, come investigate. There isn't much time.

A presence creeps over me, invisible.

"Hello?" I say, afraid to be too loud.

The forest responds with a sound I don't recognize as human or animal.

I step backward again—closer to the road, closer to my truck, my escape—and my light falls on the snow ahead of me. There are footprints I didn't make leading away from the Jetta and into the cover of trees. Along with the prints, something dark stains the fresh white. Blood. Too much of it. It disappears into the thicket near the treeline.

My thumb finds the emergency call button and I try getting through to someone who can help. The dispatcher can't hear me when I speak, so I move around, pacing circles and standing dead center in the road where the yellow line once was.

"I'm sorry. I can't understand you."

Fuck.

Another sound comes from the forest as the call ends. A voice? A cry for help. I can't tell. The wind and the engine of my truck drown out the details.

There isn't anyone else here to help, so I follow the trail away from the accident. This is Minnesota. Winter weather causes accidents all the time.

This is normal. This is normal. This. Is. Normal.

I walk through fresh, wet snow until I stand in a clearing surrounded by evergreens. The footprints end, but I don't find anyone else who could have made them.

"Hello?" I call out.

A shiver rolls up my spine, and I blame it on the numbness in my legs. I don't feel cold anymore. Whether it's from adrenaline or I've been out too long, I don't know.

I want to turn around. I mean to, but something I can't

explain draws me in. The ghosts of roots take hold of my feet and lure me deeper into the wild. The thin twigs I pass through break and snap back against my thighs, and I push away branches in my way.

This is a bad idea. Whoever crashed that car isn't out here.

But what if they are? What if I'm their only chance at going home tonight? If someone had been able to help Shelby, I would've wanted them to, so I have to do the same for this person.

A stick breaks beneath the weight of my step and I freeze. Someone moves in the brush.

"Help," a voice croaks. "Help me."

I turn in the direction of the plea. Ahead of me, in an empty space on the forest floor, a girl lies in a heap. The blood trail picks back up and leads to her, straight to a growing pool near her stomach. She looks up at me, eyes wide with terror, and begs me to help her, but I can't move away from the safety of this spot.

A tall shadow looms over her, and my light bounces off the bony claws of a hand perched on her waist. It lifts its head, but I refuse to move the flashlight upward to get a better look.

I need to shut the light off.

My arm ignores the command.

I'm frozen.

Red eyes stare forward at me, distracted for a moment from its kill. They bore through me, straight into my soul.

"Please," the girl begs. Blood bubbles up out of her mouth, and she coughs.

I can't look at her.

I can't look away.

The sound of her choking on her own blood cuts off the begging, and the shadow figure looks back down to its victim. It forgets about me, and dives forward to devour her. It gnaws the flesh from her bones with a sound like nails on a chalkboard.

TWENTY

When the fear lets me go, I run. Sticks and branches hit me hard as I move because I can't get my arms up in time to block them. Blood thrums in my ears and drowns out the sound of my boots crashing awkwardly through the snow.

My lungs burn from the cold and the exertion. The exposed skin on my cheeks and hands burns from the dry frigid air. But I don't stop until I reach my truck, locking both the doors in a frantic, flailing gesture, and peel onto the road with all the grace of an avalanche.

The truck skids at first, and I fight the physics of the slide until I right the vehicle.

I don't look back.

I can't.

When I have reception again, my call finally reaches an emergency dispatcher. I tell them about the accident and the girl in the woods, then try and explain what I saw hovering over her. What am I supposed to say? *The trees showed me where she was. She was being eaten alive by a monster. A shadow.* They won't believe any of that because I don't believe any of that.

What I saw was a trick of the light. A man with a knife. The bad lighting from my phone's flashlight stretched his shadow, turned him into something inhuman, and my brain filled in the rest.

The girl's face though... it sears itself into my mind. All the color drained from her skin, leaving her gray and cold except for the dark liquid pouring from her mouth and down onto the snow.

I couldn't have saved her.

I am not a heroine. I am not brave.

If it had been a real accident, if she had wandered out of her car and got lost—maybe then I could have helped. But this, this was beyond me.

"There was somebody in the woods. He..." I breathe. Try to, at least. "He killed her. I don't... I don't know what to do. Please send someone."

"It's going to be all right." The dispatcher's voice crackles in and out before I lose connection with them.

Paranoia takes hold of me as my mind replays the scene I saw in the clearing. My imagination superimposed red over the glistening of the figure's eyes in the light. It had no claws, only a knife, but the reality does little to ease my mind.

I saw a monster tonight, one in the form of a human made worse by the act I caught them in.

Mom's car sits in the driveway with an inch of snow collected on it already. The electronics store where she works nights must have closed early because of the weather like it does sometimes.

I shake off the things I saw in the woods. Perforated skin and dull claws—or were they knives? A girl's mouth open in an endless scream. A monster of a man devouring her. Blood.

So much blood.

The thought of it makes me sick. It coated the snow like hot, sticky syrup. Had the man's hands been covered in it? I don't remember. The lower half of his face had been, glistening in the light falling unintentionally over him.

I can't think about this right now.

When I find Mom in the kitchen with a cup of probably reheated coffee and her phone, she looks exhausted. Dark circles surround her eyes, and her skin looks heavy around the edges of her mouth. Hair hangs in limp threads past her shoulder, pulled from her braid by the wind and damp from melted snow.

"Have you heard from Shelby?" is the first thing she asks me.

"Um, no. Isn't she still in the hospital?"

Mom puts a hand over her mouth for a second before responding. Crap.

"What's going on?" I ask.

"She checked herself out earlier today." Mom inhales a shaky breath. "Your dad went to see her when he got in for his shift, and she was gone. She was supposed to stay a couple more days... and she left all her things behind."

"Oh." I check my phone, though I already know nobody texted me. "I haven't heard from her all day."

Mom unlocks her phone without lifting it from where it sits on the table and frowns at it.

"The police are looking for her."

Her gaze falls to the floor and her shoulders slump. One hand rises to push her glasses up so she can pinch her nose between her eyes, as if that ever stops anyone from crying.

"I..." I *what*? I'm not sure she's fine. I don't want to lie.

I don't know what to say to make Mom feel better, so I say nothing. Instead, I go put a hand on her shoulder as if that will fix everything.

Shelby should see what she's doing to her family. She's killing us with worry, and, since she's been home, she hasn't shown a hint of remorse for it. The way Mom looks right now—like the daughter she just got back, the daughter she thought was dead, might be gone again—is enough to make me want to slap my sister. I wonder if she would even flinch.

"I'll keep you company while you wait for her," I say.

Mom hunches forward at the kitchen table, head rested on folded arms. One hand still clutches the handle of her coffee mug. She even brewed us a fresh pot to stay awake, but the caffeine failed her somewhere around three-thirty a.m.

I, however, prop my face up with a hand and turn the page of my textbook with the other. The words have long lost their meaning now that the clock reads quarter past six.

Even Dad isn't home, but that's normal on days when the ER overflows.

The door complains as it opens, and Mom springs upright. Shelby comes in looking like she'd done nothing wrong and dressed like spring in a light canvas jacket and white sneakers without socks. Her jeans are cuffed at the ankle.

I could scream.

Mom beats me to it.

"Where the hell have you been, Shelby Jane?" Her voice carries through the house and scares the birds from their perches in trees outside. "You should have told us you were leaving the hospital. You shouldn't have left in the first place. Do you know how worried you made us?"

Shelby's expression is calm. She doesn't look like a girl on the receiving end of a mother's wrath.

"The least you could do is tell me where you're going." Mom goes from yelling to pleading.

I glare at my sister. Since she disappeared, I've had to text Mom every time I get in the truck. *Going to work. Leaving Mel's. Made it to school.* Every aspect of my life has become a compromise so I don't cause extra worry or pain. Shelby made my life like this when she vanished.

Compromise doesn't fit on Shelby, though.

"How did you get home?" Mom asks.

I hadn't heard a car pull in.

Shelby doesn't answer that question either.

"What is your problem, Shel?" I snap. "Why do you think you can do shit like this?" My voice is frayed, ragged and fringed at the edge from tiredness and frustration. "Don't you care about anyone other than yourself?"

My sister looks at me, frost around the edges of her once dark brown irises. Her expression doesn't change to show guilt or apology or anything. But with the slightest shift in posture, I notice a scar at the left corner of her chapped lips that hadn't been there before. It spreads up to her cheekbone in a jagged line, like her mouth had been torn at the edge.

"Where'd you get that scar?" I ask. It had to have been there when she first got home, and I missed it in the rush of having her back.

No reaction.

Mom reaches out to inspect the damaged skin, but Shelby flinches away.

"Don't." Shelby's voice goes low, almost a growl. "Don't touch me."

She storms back into her bedroom with those words hanging in her wake. Mom deflates back into her chair, defeated. We might have been prepared to accept that Shelby died out there, but none of us were prepared for this. It twists Mom and wrings out what little energy she has. It sends Dad deeper into his work, where he doesn't have to process the damage done. It leaves me angry.

And my sister doesn't see it. Or worse, she doesn't care.

TWENTY-ONE

Lucas stands in my checkout line with a Dr. Pepper and a package of cinnamon rolls from the bakery section. He waits behind two other customers with overflowing truck-shaped charts and toddlers about to break into a tantrum over a selection of candy they can't have.

I'd forgotten about football Sunday, a mistake I don't make during the regular season and especially not when the Vikings make the playoffs.

But, alas, here I am. Unprepared for football Sunday.

It seems everyone in the entire county either forgot or waited until the last minute to stock up on groceries for their game-day parties, because I've never seen this place as packed as it is today.

The first customer balances being pleasant to me and the boy bagging at the end of the lane with talking her toddler down from tears over the second or third candy bar she'd taken out of their hands. The kid keeps crying though, and I've never related more to a customer in my life.

I too would like to have a complete and total meltdown. The kind with screaming and crying and snots and smeared makeup. If only it wouldn't cost me my job.

The next person has an easier time keeping his child under wraps, with the compromise of sharing a Kit Kat on the ride home. I ring their groceries through without conversation, using the work as a distraction from meeting Lucas's eyes.

He came here for me, otherwise he would've gone through the self-checkout and gotten out of here ten minutes ago.

"Hey," he says, "I didn't know you worked here."

"Yes, you did." I scan the soda, then fumble with the package of cinnamon rolls. The barcode has been torn, so I type the code manually. "What do you want?"

"I need to talk to you about some stuff," he says. "You know, for our project?"

"Okay, well this isn't the place to talk about it."

He hands me a ten-dollar bill, and I count out his change.

"It's important," he says. "Can't you take a quick break? Say you have to go to the bathroom."

He pretends to recount the change I give him to buy more time, but the people behind him are getting antsy. They start scoping out other lanes to see if they'll get through faster, though they're boxed in by other customers.

Anna notices the holdup too, and gives me a look reserved for those she tolerates far less than she tolerates me.

"You need to leave. I need to get my other customers on their way too." I hold on to my composure. "Sorry about that," I say to the next customer, forcing Lucas away.

He lingers at the end of the lane, scrawling a note on his receipt, then folds it up and throws it at me. It hits me in the throat, and I flinch. The paper falls to the floor near my feet, and I cover it with my boot as a reminder to pick it up later.

"Who was that guy?" Anna sends my bagger on break and takes his place in hopes of getting new and juicy to gossip about. "He was cute."

Ugh. "Just some kid from school. He's obsessed with Bigfoot."

She keeps talking. I try not to listen.

But she gets into my head, and I type the wrong code for avocados and have to delete the entry to fix it. My hands fumble for the correct buttons, and it takes more than a few tries to get it right.

I've lost my focus.

People keep piling up at the end of the line and I want to suggest that Anna stop bothering me and go open another register, but I'm too frazzled to find the words. The customer before me frowns at my repeated mistakes, then narrows her eyes to be sure the monitor above my head shows all the right items. She points with a manicured finger at each line, then pulls it back, satisfied.

Meanwhile, I could throw up.

I sit in the breakroom with Lucas's note still folded in front of me beside a lunch I haven't touched. The turkey and cheese sandwich I'd made looks utterly unappealing to me now, probably because I still feel sick.

Things don't get in my head like that first error did

today, but it dragged me down to a place I couldn't escape. With every customer, I lost even more focus and had to fix more mistakes than I've ever made. Missed scans, erroneous produce codes, fumbled change. A disturbance crawled inside my head to throw me off my rhythm, and the job I use to shut my brain off became an inadequate distraction.

Even Anna noticed, and told me to take a break earlier than scheduled. It feels like a punishment, like I've done something horribly wrong. This can't happen again, or Anna will think I'm losing my edge now that I have what I wanted.

I wrap the sandwich back in its plastic and hide my face in my hands. All of this—Shelby, whatever the hell I saw last night, Lucas—is too much.

My sister's harsh new personality stays at the forefront of my mind and never lets me forget the spiked words she threw at me before the hospital. She hurt me to get me to do what she wanted, to get me to stop asking questions. I guess, maybe, she was always like that. I just hadn't noticed it before.

The breakroom coffeemaker sputters as it finishes brewing nearly black sludge into a paper cup. The first sip of caffeinated liquid, hot enough to cancel out even the worst flavor, straightens my brain out. I force myself to eat half the sandwich. It tastes like nothing, like cardboard spread with cheap mayonnaise. It does nothing but add weight to my stomach.

Then I finally open the receipt Lucas threw at me, brushing bits of dirt left behind from my boot. Oh, what I wouldn't give for him to tell me he can fix this.

Text me on your break. We need to talk.

I hesitate before entering his number, but giving him

mine can't be worse than him showing up and causing trouble at my work.

I can ignore my phone.

It's Cara. I have five minutes. What do you want?

While I wait for a response, I stare up at the sports coverage playing on the tiny screen mounted in one corner of the room.

Meet me at Eleanor's after your shift.

Eleanor's is the only place left in town to go. It's some cross between a diner, a cafe, a bar, a general store, and an antiquated gas station. The woman in charge, whose name is not Eleanor, but Peg, keeps it running by serving everything anyone could possibly want.

The place thrives while everything else collapses around it.

That's the thing about living in a dying town. No one wants to accept that it's dying until it's too far gone. First, the second-rate chain restaurants close—shutting their doors one night, never to see another customer—and then the better ones disappear the same way until the main drag becomes a ghost town of buildings that were once Pizza Huts and Wendy's.

The strongest place remains, flourishes, because locals approve of it. It's the place for birthday parties and first dates, for important meetings and unimportant ones.

Eleanor's is that place.

So while this town is well into its death sentence, business continues as usual there. We may not have our old hardware stores and doctor's offices like we used to, but we have Eleanor's. We have the nostalgia that comes with it.

Fine. I'm out at five. I know I asked him for help, but I can't ignore how annoying he is.

Great. See you there.

My hands tremble as I stuff the phone and remaining half sandwich into my bag. The coffee may have cleared my head, but it left the rest of me shaky and uneasy. Stomach acid sloshes around the meager offering I gave it like it wants to reject it. A shaky feeling other than nerves hangs over me now, like frozen hands closing around my lungs, my heart.

TWENTY-TWO

I find Lucas at Eleanor's in a booth in the corner with a basket of cut veggies and dip set in front of him. He sits with a carrot between two fingers like a cigarette, creamy ranch dripping off the end, and his opposite hand scrolling through thick blocks of text on a laptop. He looks focused. I almost don't want to disturb him.

Except I need him to tell me what he knows so we can get this over with. I need him to do the job he said he could do.

"Hey." I sit across from him. "Work kept me late. Sorry"

The apology doesn't feel right on my tongue. Did I really just apologize to Lucas Powell?

"It's fine. Research kept me busy." He leans over to the chair beside him and digs through his bag until he retrieves a folder. "I have the contract for you to sign, then we can get to work."

My eyes bulge at the contract. It's only a few pages long, but it looks official. Am I hiring a hitman?

"What the hell? If I sign all this, you won't like... take my parents' house or anything, right?"

Lucas goes through each page, showing me where to sign and what I'm agreeing to. The short version is that I'm agreeing to cooperate with him and any other hunters he may recruit for the assignment, that I will not talk about anything regarding the assignment with anyone, and that I will not post anything on social media about it. Easy enough.

"Like I said before, if you do go public with any of this, there are consequences. Think witness protection, except you don't get to talk to anyone anymore and people back home think of you... well, kind of how you think of me."

"Like a lunatic?" I say before I can catch myself.

He frowns. "Exactly."

"Fabulous." I sign each place he tells me to.

One of Peg's part-time employees, a girl I recognize vaguely from school, comes by to take my order and to ask Lucas if he needs anything else. I order fries and a regular coffee. Lucas asks for half an order of fried cheese curds.

"Okay, so I've signed your contract. I'm not going to talk to anyone about this. So what can you do? What have you figured out?"

I wish it wasn't weird to sit next to him so I could see the screen, but it would definitely be weird.

"Are you going to hit me again when I start talking?"

"No."

"I should have put a line in the contract about that."

I roll my eyes. "I swear on my cat's life that I will not punch you again." I hold up a hand as though swearing an oath. Lucas doesn't catch the sarcasm in my tone or gesture, and offers half a smile in response.

"Okay. Well based on the descriptions from people at the party, the animal attacks around when Shelby vanished, and how you've said Shelby's been acting, I've narrowed it down to a few creatures."

Creatures. Great.

"We can rule out Sasquatch. He's big, but not aggressive to people. If anyone had spotted him, he'd be long gone by now."

"Okay..." I pause, fight the urge to roll my eyes again. "What else is there? Vampires? Werewolves?"

Lucas frowns. "Werewolves are a category of creatures that encompass many individuals. In our region, we have Wolfman, but he rarely stands on his hind legs. Even if he does, he only reaches six or seven feet in height. Everyone said what they saw had to be at least ten."

His words give me the chills. I hate them. I hate this. There is no such thing as the goddamn Wolfman.

"And vampires never really, I guess, caught on in the Americas. They're mostly in Europe still."

"Fine. Okay. No vampires then." Annoyance bubbles up in me, creating a buildup of murderous sarcasm. "Maybe it's Lizard Man. Remember, everyone said he'd come out during that eclipse back in 2017?"

"Doubtful. Reptilian creatures tend to stay south, where it's warm. Same reason we don't have alligators up here."

I groan. "Just tell me what you think it is, Lucas. I don't care about the biology lesson."

He shifts in his seat, eats a piece of broccoli before answering.

"I just need you to know something before we continue. These things are dangerous. My family has centuries of knowledge and skills passed down to us from the founders of the hunters. This isn't going to be anything like hunting a violent bear or even the smartest serial killer, Cara. Some of the tracking will be similar, but that's where the parallels end."

"Okay. I understand." I think that's what he wants me to say. I hope so.

He picks at another piece of broccoli, dunks it in the ranch, glances back at the kitchen to see if our server is on her way back yet.

"Have you heard of the Iceheart?"

"No. No, I most definitely have not." I can't. I can't deal with this. This is absurd.

But still, I step deeper into Lucas's world. One step closer to the point of no return, where I have to either believe him or see myself out of the rabbit hole alone.

"What is it?" I ask, even though I really don't want to know.

TWENTY-THREE

Our food arrives and I pluck a fry from the basket and dunk it in the container of ketchup on the side. The fry's still too hot, but I hold the bite in my mouth and breathe around it. Lucas does the same thing with one of his cheese curds. It's an unspoken rule that it's better to suffer through the heat than spit the food out.

Besides, the burning feeling gives me something to focus on other than the monster Lucas was ready to tell me about. The Iceheart? It sounds made up. It sounds fake.

"It's a malevolent spirit. Non-corporeal. It latches onto someone and, eventually, takes their body as its own. You ever hear of the fungus *ophiocordyceps unilateralis?*"

I scrunch my face, crinkling the skin on my nose.

"A fungus? You think Shelby's being stalked by a mushroom?"

He shakes his head. "No. I'm saying the Iceheart works like the fungus does. Sort of. The fungus takes over the bodies of ants in the Amazon and drives them mad. Once they lose control, the fungus makes them climb to a certain height, then spores burst from the ant's head and spread to other ants."

I look at him with my mouth half open. Like, what the hell, Lucas?

"The Iceheart spirit behaves similarly. It waits quietly, safely anchored in an object like a tree while it waits for a human host to possess. Once it has a host, it drives them out of their mind until it has full control over them. It doesn't spread itself like the *cordyceps* does. But it needs the body to attempt to satisfy its insatiable hunger."

"Great." Obviously not great, but what else can I say? "What makes you think this is our monster?" I feel foolish for asking the question, for validating his belief that this creature of his is the problem.

"The animal attacks in the woods, for one. They're inconsistent with the predators around here, and no human could be as uh, thorough in their work."

I had heard Emily's and Parker's bodies were only identifiable by dental records or something, but I tried not to think about it. Not with Shelby out there, possibly another victim.

"Okay, fine. Say I believe you. Say we go for this. What's next?"

"We need to rule out other monsters, prove this is our guy, and then we make our moves. Right now, we investigate. Everything you learn from Shelby, you tell me. I have a few leads I can follow on my end."

Investigating sounds time consuming. It sounds like a waste of energy, but this is Lucas's speciality—assuming I choose to believe him—so I don't argue.

We eat our food for a bit in silence. I don't know what to say next. I don't want to volunteer for any of his investigating, whatever that entails.

"You've heard of the Winter Tree, right?"

I roll my eyes so far back, my vision goes dark for a minute. Honestly, I can't help it. Listening to him talk about monsters is enough for one day. I don't need to hear the county's only notable story for the nine millionth time.

"So you know the tree is preserved perfectly despite having been dead for centuries?"

I nod.

"There is a theory among my colleagues—"

Colleagues. He said *colleagues* like he's some kind of business man or developer or whatever. I understand now why people drink.

"—that the Iceheart is linked to that tree. It would account for the lack of decay of the remains, and for the unexplained deaths surrounding it. People get too close on a dare, it takes one as host, eats the others. Then the host body dies and the spirit returns to the tree."

"Shelby went to the tree before she disappeared, but she didn't die." I poke holes in his story.

"They don't always. Plenty of people survive. The Iceheart lives in its host, abandoning the tree for a time."

"Okay, so then maybe this isn't the right monster. Maybe she just left and, I don't know, started doing drugs. I wouldn't put it past her, really. She needed help."

He taps his fingers on the laptop's keyboard only loud enough to make a gentle clicking sound.

"This is why we need to find more information before we jump to any conclusions."

I lean back in my chair and stare past Lucas. My fries have gone cold, but I keep eating them to pass the time it takes to process all the thoughts in my head. Every cell in my body resists the idea that this monster could possibly be real.

"How does this explain what people say they've seen? No human is ten feet tall. And if it takes regular people as hosts..."

Lucas leans forward on his elbows, shutting the laptop as if it hides things I shouldn't know about yet. He meets my gaze with eyes full of something I can't quite place. Sympathy? Remorse? Regret? I don't know him well enough to read it.

"Once in possession of a host, it can... shift. Uh, change its physical form to be more equipped for hunting."

I draw in a shaking breath. What he tells me can't be true. He relays elaborate works of fiction spun as reality.

"Its shifted form is stronger than your average human. Faster. Self-healing. And narrow as the trunks of the trees it hides among."

The thing he describes is beyond impossible.

"The hosts don't last long. Their organs are preserved in some kind of stasis, but the stress of transforming like that takes a toll. Usually they only last a few days. If they survive weeks, physical destruction becomes visible—scars, unhealed wounds, chapped lips, peeling skin. Only a few hosts in history have lasted longer than a few months."

I can't talk about this anymore. I don't need more details about this monster. Not now, while we have so much left to do.

"How will you get the information you need? I can tell you what happened leading up to Shelby leaving, if that helps."

Lucas shrugs like maybe it'll help, but he has a different idea. "I'll work backward from the day she returned, try and piece together where she could have been. Check police reports for other animal attacks. Scope out the woods for evidence the spirit has left the tree. Stuff like that."

"Do you have a partner in this? Like cops and stuff usually do?"

"No. The hunters are stretched thin as it is with so few of us for so many territories. My dad's gone, and my mom can't do the work in her condition. It's all me. This territory is my responsibility."

It almost seems unfair to saddle him with the fate of an entire community.

"I'll help."

He looks at me, surprised. Neither of us expected this, but the offer has been made and now I can't take it back.

Lucas Powell has agreed to help me, sure, but I still can't believe I just said I'd help him.

TWENTY-FOUR

More snow comes down, this time heavy enough to convince the district to give us a two-hour delay. I watch the snow fall from the kitchen table beside, and clutch a warm cup of coffee between both hands. Charlie usually sits with me in the rare, slow mornings, but, since Shelby's come back, the two of them have made their dislike for one another abundantly clear. Charlie stays in my room now, only leaving to use her litterbox in the bathroom and to hiss at Shelby when the opportunity arises.

"You want a cup?" I ask Shelby, tilting my head toward the coffee pot.

She shakes her head. "No. Too hot."

My sister turns her attention back to the window, white hair hanging on either side of her face.

"It's pretty out there," she says.

She used to hate the cold. The snow. Everything about Minnesota, but especially the rural north. The summers were too short. Wolf County was too sleepy. The things we have here, the harvest festivals and county fairs, were beneath her. She wanted live music. She wanted art. She wanted the exact opposite of this place.

"Did you miss it?" I ask. "The snow?"

She doesn't meet my eyes. Whatever happened to her, it makes her shy away from my gaze, from everyone's. She always finds something else to look at, something to distract her, so she won't have to look at us.

The doctors think it's a response to trauma, but no one can pinpoint exactly what kind.

Maybe she avoids our gaze because she worries we'll find the truth in her eyes.

"It was prettier where I went," she says. "You could walk for days and never see another person. Just the forest. It was the end of the Earth, and it belonged to me."

"You hate the cold." I take advantage of her talkative mood in hopes of prying information from her. "Why not go somewhere warm? Like you planned?"

She looks vaguely in my direction, eyes settling on an object on the counter behind me. Her face rests in a tired expression, hanging heavy and dull over jagged cheek-bones. What I thought was makeup when she arrived home still circles her eyes, dark and hollow.

"The heat is too heavy. Like being drowned on land and boiled alive all at once. The ice and snow are more comfort-able to me now."

I watch her mouth, watch the movement of speech shift the scarred skin from the corner of her lips to her cheek. What could have caused that? A burn, maybe?

The sting of my own broken skin indicates I've picked too much at the edges of my nail, but I don't stop. The pain grounds me to this moment, where Shelby has chosen to open up.

"Why won't you tell me where you went?" If she

doesn't like the heat, then where? Alaska? Northern Canada? I can't picture her bundled in a heavy jacket and mittens and scarves. I can't imagine her embracing the cold.

"There's nothing to tell. It wasn't much different from this."

"Did somebody hurt you?" I ask.

"There was nobody to hurt me, Cara. I was alone. More alone than you can imagine."

I reach for her wrist to comfort her, but she yanks her arm away. She isn't the only one who knows what it feels like to be alone. The way the loneliness eats away at you until your insides feel hollow. The way it constantly aches to remind you nothing will ever fill that emptiness.

"Why did you leave, Shel? Why did you do this to us?" I speak low to hide the agony in my voice. She single-handedly shattered this family on her way out. We tried to put ourselves back together, but some of the pieces are missing and cracks will always show.

"I didn't have a choice."

She pulls her knees up to her chest in a way that reminds me so much of who she was. The pressure of her body curled up like that must be comforting, like rolling into the fetal position beneath the covers to hide from the sounds the walls make in the wind.

"Of course you had a choice."

"No. You don't understand yet. You will."

I lean back against my chair and prop an elbow on the table. I wish the police were here, or even my parents. They'd know what questions to ask, while I'd already run out. I don't know what else to say.

"What made you talk to me today?"

Her eyes meet mine for the first time since I found her at

the kitchen table, and it sends ice through my veins. Hidden in the specks of frost mixed with brown, a mysterious presence hides. It doesn't mean well. It claws at her, a sickness fighting to expose itself to the world.

I see it inside her, plain as day.

"I don't get to choose anymore. All I can do is hope I have the strength to stay in control for a little while."

The wind changes outside from the bluster of a snowstorm to a wicked and unrelenting blizzard. It whips off the side of the house with a violent scream. Where there had once been brightness between the snowflakes, a dark gray creeps in.

"Is it drugs? Is that it?" It would explain so much, I think. But the hospital would have found something. They did so many tests, they would have told us if it were something like that. "Nobody will be angry if you tell the truth."

She shakes her head, slow and certain.

"I'm trying to help you. Why don't you understand that? Why bother coming home if you don't want our support?"

My sister's posture changes in a snap. She drops her feet to the floor and sits up straight. Her expression changes from the look a person gets when they don't have the energy to hold their facial muscles up to something sharper.

"The only way you can help me is to kill me."

TWENTY-FIVE

S helby and I ate lunch together at school and didn't talk about how she was clearly avoiding her friends and Parker. A couple times, I planned to ask her about it—I almost did—but every time I came close, she sensed it and started a different conversation.

"Is it really that expensive to buy real pizza, do you think?" Shelby frowned at the not-quite-melted cheese atop the square slice of previously frozen pizza. It didn't look appetizing.

"You should know by now not to get that. You'll never not be disappointed by it," I said.

She looked past me, a scowl deepening a line between her eyebrows. "Speaking of disappointed..."

I turned and saw Emily coming our way. Ugh. Shit. I still wasn't sure if Shelby had a full on friend breakup or if she was just ignoring them for a while until she stopped being mad. Either way, I was pretty sure the interaction would end badly.

"Shel! God, where have you been?" Emily asked.

My sister kept her head low, and glared up at Emily. "Here."

"Okay, duh. But like, what is going on? Why weren't you at the—"

Someone yelled something across the cafeteria and cut Emily off, but we all knew what word came at the end of that sentence. *Why weren't you at the party?* It suggested there had been another party Shelby didn't get invited to.

I held onto the remaining half of my turkey sandwich with both hands, like the stale bread and flavorless turkey would see me through the storm to come.

"We're already planning Halloween!" Emily said. "I think it's time we make the hike to the Winter Tree. You know, leave our mark here before we leave Wolf County."

Shelby's chestnut hair hid most of her expression, but the redness in her cheeks stood out from where I sat.

"Why did you come over here?" Shelby asked.

"Uh, to talk to you about Halloween. It won't be the same without you."

"Right. Of course." Shelby looked up, more sad than angry, and met Emily's eyes. "Were the last two weekends the same without me? Did you know that Parker told me one was canceled because his dad was using the cabin? Did he make you keep a secret this weekend so I wouldn't feel bad?"

Emily frowned. "I thought you were invited and just wanted a break."

"I'm not stupid, you know."

As if he knew what was happening based on the tension radiating off this table, Parker showed up in the empty seat beside Shelby.

"Hey. Missed you on Saturday," he said, like nothing was wrong. Like my sister wasn't near her breaking point.

"Are you fucking kidding me?" Shelby snapped. "Seriously, I want to know. Is this a joke? Do you really think nothing's wrong? You lied to me."

She slammed a plastic knife down into the center of her pizza, and it stood up straight.

Parker held his hands up and leaned away from Shelby's reach, as if a few inches would matter if she decided to hit him.

"I thought you needed a break. You seemed to be going downhill," he said.

Shelby laughed. I hated the sound of it. Bitter and cold and humorless.

"Then talk to me, Parker. Don't go behind my back as if I won't find out. Do you really think this entire school isn't always talking about your parties? It's the one thing to do in this entire state." She didn't inhale between the words. "I'm really done. I don't need any of you."

Parker stood up and took a place beside Emily. They looked like they wanted to retreat, but didn't dare.

Shelby caught her breath and tore the knife from her pizza, turning her attention back to cutting it into bite-sized pieces. The flush of red drained from her face and she resumed her meal, like nothing had happened.

I looked at her friends—former friends, I guess—and waited for them to do something. To say something. To try and justify excluding her with something better than Parker's half-assed explanation. Shelby deserved to know why her friends lied to her.

Emily started to speak, but stopped before the words ever had meaning. Parker remained silent, deliberate.

It felt like an eternity passed before someone finally decided what to say.

"We're worried about you," Parker said.

I didn't know what those parties had turned into since Shelby stopped asking me to go with her, but Shelby had always been a little out of control. Why stop her now?

Shelby didn't like the answer, because she lifted her head again to acknowledge the presence of Parker and Emily. Of me, even. With one swift motion, she flung her entire tray off the table. It hit Parker in the thigh, then tumbled to the ground—pizza and utensils and everything.

"I'll give you something to worry about." She stood and took her bag, then strolled right past a group of teachers and out of the cafeteria.

TWENTY-SIX

A hand finds my arm and yanks me into a cove of lockers and out of the herd of students moving through the hallways.

Once I regain my bearings, I find Lucas standing in front of me.

"Don't touch me again. Ever," I snap. "We clear?"

The sound of boots squeaking against dry spots on the linoleum and slipping against wet ones changes the feel of the school. Sleeves of puffy jackets swish against the sides. People shake the snow out of their hair, their hats, everywhere it collects when given the chance, then discard damp outer layers into their lockers. The snow day creates a familiar scene where everyone here has forgotten, just this once and just for a few moments, about everything but warming up and drying off.

"Sorry."

I shift the weight of my bag onto my opposite shoulder and cross my arms. "What do you want?"

"You haven't heard about the missing junior?" Lucas asks.

"I don't have a TV at home, and you're the first person I've talked to today. So, no. I haven't heard."

"She's been missing since Saturday."

The day stands out in my mind, along with all the horrific details.

"She was at that party a couple weeks ago where everyone saw the uh, monster in the woods. I think..." He lowers his voice as a boy opens a locker near us.

The boy dumps all his stuff inside, takes a single notepad and a pen, then heads back into the stampede.

"... iIt could be related."

"Oh." Too many thoughts bombard me at once. A trickle of sweat rolls from my underarm to the band of my bra, and I flap my arms like wings to dry myself. "What time did she disappear?"

Lucas taps his lower lip, thinking. "She left her dad's house in Riverside around five on Saturday and never got to her mom's in Wolf Hill."

I close my eyes. "Was she driving a silver Volkswagen?"

There it goes. Out in the world. No coming back from this now.

Lucas pales. "I thought you said—"

"I did. I didn't hear about it."

My stomach goes sick, sour like curdled milk. What I wouldn't give for her to have been driving anything else. Then this wouldn't be my problem.

"I already knew about it." Could incriminate me somehow. Probably not? "I found the accident. I tried to help. I... I called it in."

His jaw drops. "You did what? Why didn't you tell me?"

There are plenty of answers to that question. The accident had nothing to do with him. Whatever I saw in the woods was human. I didn't want to think about how Shelby could be involved in this. It was a regular thing that happens sometimes in the north when it snows.

But instead of answering his question like a reasonable human being, like someone who asked him for help, I choose to be a dick about it.

"I didn't realize I needed to keep a diary for you."

He frowns.

"Tell me everything you saw. Do you remember where you saw the car? We'll talk on the way there."

"What? No. I can tell you where it is, but I can't go anywhere. I have class."

"I need you to take me, Cara. You signed a contract to work with me. This could be important."

I had a feeling I'd regret signing that piece of paper.

"You want my soul too then?"

He doesn't laugh. He wins though.

NOT FIVE MINUTES LATER, he sits in the passenger's seat firing questions at me faster than I can answer, and scribbles notes in his notebook. On his insistence that the things I've seen could have something to do with Shelby, I tell him everything from the beginning.

I tell him about the night at Mel's when I saw the person in the brush, about how I keep feeling like someone's watching me. He listens when I tell him about how Charlie acted the night Shelby came home and how she still acts strange around her.

He listens, but he says nothing.

As I speak, I focus on a strip of lazy, brown sand trailing down the center of the road. I claim it for myself, aligning my chunky tires where the snow thins out.

"What did you see out here? Anything?"

Lucas turns down the radio without my permission, and it annoys the hell out of me even though I haven't been listening to it.

I turn it back up.

"Nothing really. I saw the accident. There was blood on the steering wheel, but no driver. Then I found the footprints and a little"—it was *not* little—"trail of blood leading away. It was dark though. Couldn't see past my nose."

"Try and remember."

"Okay, but what do you think I'm doing?"

"Did you see the victim? Was she with anyone?"

The details of the night blur around the edges, reality mixing with logic. I take a moment to ground myself. "She was with a man." A man with a knife. Human, barely. "She was bleeding bad, and I don't know if he was helping or…"

I stop to focus on guiding the truck to a stop on the shoulder where I found the Jetta. The only sign of it now, after the layer of fresh snow, is a mark on a tree where the bumper scraped at the bark. The girl's footprints have long been lost among those of police and search parties.

The forest wants me to remember the way. It guides me, gently, into its cover. So gently, I might think I was making the decision on my own. But I wouldn't go, not if I weren't pulled like this.

Lucas and I weave through the woods and snow. It feels familiar.

The trees swallow us whole, funneling us not to their stomach, but to their heart—a clearing with caution tape set up in a circle. The snow here has been more obviously disturbed, and the ground shows the spot where something, someone was dragged away. A dark smudge, maybe blood or maybe dirt, stains the edges of snow in places.

It makes my stomach turn, and memories bombard me. Imaginary monsters tearing into a girl. A ghost of a man crouched over her on the forest floor, knife in hand. Her face distorted mid-scream as her blood spills on the frozen ground.

"What happened here?" I ask.

I need him to pick the truth out of the mess of images in my head and tell me what he sees there. To tell me there wasn't a monster.

"You tell me," he says.

"I don't know. I told you, I don't know what I saw."

My eyes pinch shut against flashes of that night. Blood. Knives. Claws. *Agony.* I would give anything to erase them from my head.

Lucas frowns. "The report said the caller said there was an attacker. If you called it in, then... did you think the man beside her was hurting her?"

"I don't remember what I saw. I didn't want to come out here."

I stop myself right before I tell him the trees compelled me to walk to this place. He doesn't need to know that.

He takes a pair of black nitrile gloves out of his pocket and pulls them on, then kneels beside the edge of the brush.

"What are you doing?" I swallow. Gloves seem legit. "Don't tell me you're looking for broken sticks with blood on them or whatever."

Lucas scoffs. "That's fiction. Even if it weren't, the snow would have ruined any trail like that."

I throw my hands up. "Of course. What was I thinking?"

The silence settles into my bones while I wait for Lucas

to speak again. I don't know what to do out here, so I don't do anything.

When he turns too slowly, my stomach drops. Nobody turns like that unless they caught that prickling sensation of something watching, something too close, and they don't want to scare it off before they can catch a glimpse.

Then he rises and disappears into the overgrowth.

Shit.

I follow him, because being alone out here seems worse than trying to physically catch a murderer.

When the trees clear again after I've lost track of how long we've been walking, I find Lucas digging through his backpack. He removes a small, black digital camera and kneels beside something I can't get a good look at from here.

A few steps forward, clarity comes chased by regret.

I cover my hand with my mouth and swallow the sound that tries to pass my lips. Despite the temperature, sweat darts to my palms and the heat of adrenaline keeps me alive. My knees go weak, and I catch myself on a nearby aspen.

A pile of bones, snapped in half and cast aside, lies in the stained snow before me.

LUCAS INSPECTS the fragments of bone in his gloved fingers, and I watch. I should look away, but he keeps talking to himself and I keep thinking he's talking to me. Now, I watch as he works like he knows a thing or two about investigating dead bodies.

Looking at the remains, I can't confirm whether these

belong to the girl I'd seen in the woods two nights ago. I don't think anyone could.

"Lucas..." I begin, "how......?"

"They may have died at the end of a knife, or by the impact of a bullet, or by any of a million ways, but it didn't end there. They were torn apart so thoroughly, there were barely scraps left for the coyotes."

Oh my god.

"Even the marrow is gone." He holds up one of the larger pieces as if to show me, but I don't want to see. "And you can see teeth marks."

I raise my hands, cover my eyes.

The thought of teeth scraping against bone sends this morning's coffee back up, past my lips, and onto the snow.

How does this happen?

"We need to call the police."

"No. No, I'll handle this," Lucas insists.

I shake my head. "No. We have to report the body found. Their family needs to know. They deserve closure."

He tries again to protest, but I've started walking back to the road so I can look for enough reception to call. The only thing I care about for a little while is letting the police know so this person's family can get answers. It doesn't matter if the bones belong to the girl I saw or someone else. Someone must be waiting for them. Family. Friends. A partner.

THE POLICE SUGGEST in no uncertain terms that Lucas and I return to the Wolf County Sheriff's Office. We found a dead body not far from a crime scene. Now we have to answer questions, and oh god, the floor swims beneath my feet when I pass the threshold to the station.

Dad sits with a woman Lucas points out as his mother. She has a black cane propped up against a leg, and she doesn't speak. She looks at her son with questioning, but doesn't grill him. Not like Dad does the second he lays eyes on me.

"What are you doing? Skipping class? Wandering the woods in the middle of a storm? Near a crime scene? Cara, you know better," Dad says in a single breath. "Is this about your sister? Do you need more support from your mom and I? What's going on?"

He glances at Lucas, not bothering to comment on my company.

"It's just," I begin. I can tell him the truth. Some of it, at least. "I think what happened to that girl might be about Shelby. Or she might be involved somehow. It can't be a coincidence."

"Then tell the police what you know and let them do their job. People die in these woods, Cara, and I can't have it be you next time."

Dad's words sting, but I deserve them.

Lucas may be some kind of bounty hunter/assassin/monster hunter, but I'm not. I'm a cashier at a supermarket and sometimes I babysit kittens. Nothing in my experience qualifies me for this. That won't stop me though.

"I'm sorry." ...*That I got caught.* "I don't know what I was thinking." At least that part isn't quite a lie.

"Answer their questions and go straight back to school," Dad says. "If this continues, we take your keys."

"Yeah, okay. Then you can drive me to school and to

Mel's and to work. Or, I could quit my job and give up the internship I got. Would that be preferable to you?"

He looks at me, wide-eyed. At first, I think it's because I rarely talk back, but then I realize I never told them I was chosen for the internship. Never had the chance.

Before he can respond, I set my jaw and go to the door where a deputy has called for us.

Lucas and I follow when he leads us down the hallway, then the deputy guides me to a room alone for questioning. He leaves me with a female deputy whose name tag reads *Oliver*, then he and Lucas continue on their way.

The room feels too hot, and I tug at the collar of my sweater while the cop on the other side of the table introduces herself.

"Let's start with the easy stuff. What were you and your friend doing in the woods?" she asks.

"Sometimes we just need to get some fresh air." I repeat the answer Lucas and I rehearsed before the police arrived at the scene. He knew they'd separate us. He seems to know a lot about this kind of thing.

Deputy Oliver doesn't buy it. It shows in the way her perfect eyebrows curve and her mouth straightens. It was a bad lie. It's January.

"Ms. Hughes, did Mr. Powell take you into the woods against your will?"

I blanche.

"What? No. No, of course not. I drove."

She writes something down. "Were you in any way coerced into going with him to such a remote area?"

"No," I say. Lucas sucks, but he's the annoying kind of terrible. Not the kind to take me out into the woods and force himself on me. At least, I'm pretty sure. "It's not like that. He didn't lay a hand on me."

"Okay, so you two weren't fooling around. Why else would you be in the woods in January? And don't try and tell me you were getting some air."

I hold back an eye roll at the words *fooling around*. Who even says that anymore? Besides, this county is tiny. Surely the deputy, like everyone, knows Lucas is not my type.

"We didn't want to be in school. I wanted the quiet."

"And you just wind up finding a girl who'd gone missing barely days ago? You know how that looks, right?"

I frown. "You can't be serious."

The blood in my veins turns to lead, and I become so heavy the cheap, metal chair threatens to give out beneath me. Does she really think I could have done this?

As if reading my mind, she pulls a sheet of paper from a plain manila folder and turns it so I can read it. She taps a finger on a familiar number. *My* phone number.

"Is it a coincidence you were at the scene on Saturday then? That is your phone number, isn't it?"

Don't panic, Cara. Don't. Panic.

"I was driving home from work at the supermarket."

She urges me on.

"I saw the car off the road and went to see if anyone had been hurt. All the doors were open." I catch my own inconsistency after it's too late. Only one door had been open. My heart pounds. "I thought someone might have been disoriented and went off into the woods."

"Why didn't you call the police first?"

"I tried. I did. The reception was too bad." The truth comes so effortlessly, because she'll believe it. Cell reception in these woods is always a gamble. "When I saw the blood, I wanted to try and help."

"And what did you find?"

The woman's blue eyes bore holes in me, as if she

wonders what I plan to say. I tell her what I told the dispatcher.

"I don't remember. I found the girl, but there was a man with her too. I think... I think he... " I pause to breathe. "I think he killed her."

It was a man.

Lucas may have some real skills when it comes to crime scenes, but there are still no monsters.

Though, at this moment, something else flashes in my mind. Eyes glowing like stoplights in a fog. Claws like jagged bones grown straight through fingertips. Insatiable hunger in the form of a monster. A killer.

My body tenses as if I'm being attacked.

"The accident didn't kill her." I try to sound more confident. "Something else did."

The deputy frowns. "Did you see the killer's face? Anything?"

"No." I glance back at my number on the paper. "He was tall. Skinny. That's all I saw."

"Did he see you?"

"I don't think so." Would he have let me go if he had?

The door creaks open and one of the deputies I recognize from the hospital—Deputy Mendes—enters with a grim expression on her face. She whispers something to her colleague then takes a seat. She eyes me with skepticism.

"So, after all that, why would you come back to the scene of the accident? How did you find the remains that deputies and search parties couldn't find?"

"We weren't looking for them. I just... I thought I could help. I thought I could find her if I went back." It's a bad answer, but I don't have a better one.

Deputy Mendes takes over the questioning. "Are you

under the impression that the police are unable to handle this case?"

"No. Of course not."

"Then I suggest you direct your focus on your school-work and let us do our job. You do think we are capable of doing our job, don't you?"

Honestly, no. But her question is not the kind to be answered truthfully. "Yes, ma'am."

"The two of you should go back to school now. I don't want to hear another word from either of you for the duration of this investigation."

A visible jolt of anxiety levels me, and the deputies notice my attempt to hide it.

"I understand you want to help because of your sister, but you need to stay out of this."

TWENTY-SEVEN

Lucas rides with me back to school, and thankfully the drive is short so I don't have to listen to every detail of his conversation with the police. He alternates between asking if they'd asked me the same questions as him and asking about what exactly I saw when I called the accident in. I don't feel like talking about it.

When we get to school, sick curiosity tears through the halls as if the person who died—who someone *killed*—had been nothing more than a prop. The people who don't panic stand in clusters and spin the situation into elaborate lies.

They speak loud enough to be overheard, and maybe they want it that way. They talk about how Lucas and I found bones with flesh peeled away and marrow sucked dry, and how the police can't even identify the body. Fear laces the words, but everyone pretends they aren't scared of the fact that, sometimes, stuff like this happens in our woods.

I don't know where they got the information so fast. The police wouldn't have released the gruesome details.

Then, talk of the remains we found mingles with week-old gossip about Shelby. People spout perceived similarities and connections as if they've been trained to such things.

"You know, the last thing Shelby Hughes did before she disappeared was go to the Tree. Maybe she was supposed to die, and the Tree wants the blood she owes it," a boy says. Everyone around him nods in agreement.

"If it wants her blood, why not just kill her? She's here," a girl says.

"I don't know, but maybe we should sacrifice her to it. Give it what it wants," the first boy continues.

"Don't you think cutting it down would be easier?" a second boy asks.

"Less bloody, too," another kid says. They move a few steps away from the boy who suggested sacrifice, as if the boy might try to sacrifice whoever's closest.

"That won't work if it's possessed."

The group continues to go through all the ways killing my sister will solve the town's problems.

Their conversation stirs up Shelby's words from the other night. *The only way you can help me is to kill me.*

No. I will not allow the thought to settle. I push it away. These people are wrong. Shelby is a victim. She deserves to heal, not be sacrificed to an allegedly bloodthirsty, possessed tree by a couple scared teenagers.

"Well, I heard Cara and Lucas found the body. Maybe they did it. Cara has a motive, right?" someone asks. "Maybe she asked him to help offer another person to the Tree in exchange for her sister. Maybe that's what happened to Emily Jardin last year. An offering."

People mutter amongst themselves, and I feel them watching me. For the rest of Monday and all of Tuesday, whispers follow me around the school. I let them cling to my back like parasites, let them latch onto my skin and suck out my soul.

By the time Lucas catches me at my locker, I've grown numb to the world around me.

Mom doesn't want me talking to him. She doesn't want him planting ideas in my head about Shelby's situation. Or worse, pulling me out of school to search for missing girls. I don't know how to tell her I asked him for help, because it means telling her what I've seen.

I don't know how to begin to tell her the truth.

"Please tell me what you really saw in the woods. Please, Cara."

When we went our separate ways yesterday, I left with only the story I told the police—that the killer was human. I could tell him about the images creeping into my head. The claws, the blood, the teeth. I could tell him. But they linger like a bad taste.

"What can you do about it? You think we're up against something you've never fought. We can't stop this, Lucas."

"Yes, we can. What do I have to do to prove to you that I'm not making this monster stuff up. What do I have to gain by telling you this shit?"

I slam my locker door so hard the metal vibrates beneath my palm. "Tell me your plan. How do you hunt this thing?"

He frowns. "I don't have a plan yet. We're still in the investigation phase."

My head rolls back and the bones in my neck crack. The lights on the ceiling leave little white orbs of color—orange and pink and yellow—when I look back to Lucas.

"What more is there to investigate? Ugh... Some monster hunter you are." My tone mocks him.

He recoils, wounded. "It isn't a common monster. It

has an extremely limited range given its aversion to heat, especially with global temperatures rising, and it prefers to lure its victims in rather than venturing into populated areas to hunt. If this is an Iceheart, its behavior is unusual."

"So, what? Has anyone killed one of these things?" I ask, forcing myself to sound genuine. This is a waste of time.

"I don't know. All I know is a lot of good hunters have died because of it."

I slide my phone from my pocket and open a text to my parents—*staying late at the library*—and focus on the screen so he won't see my face.

"Cara—"

"I'm leaving now. Go investigate."

I can't focus on my assignment. The document taunts me from the library computer screen, barely touched. The handwritten version sits beside me, neglected, though the whole reason I came here was to type the assignment for submission. Well, and to escape Lucas.

Behind the document, a browser tempts me with all the stories it could tell.

I tap the screen on my silenced phone to see if I have any messages. Part of me hopes Lucas has something to share, that he went out to find the answers he should have by now. I could text him, but I don't.

I have my own shit to deal with.

Curiosity wins eventually though, and I click the browser behind my assignment and type the word Iceheart into the search bar. Dozens of results come up, but it all centers around monsters in video games and horror movies. Nothing useful. So I try searching for Wolf County folklore instead.

There is nothing about the monster, but I find a website that catches my attention: the story of the Winter Tree.

I click the link and lean back in my chair to read the contents of the post, written by a resident of Montville whose last name sounds familiar.

The Winter Tree is a decades-old tree that has been preserved in death for almost a century. The Winter Tree stands among a thriving forest in the unincorporated territories within Wolf County, Minnesota. It is said that the dark spirit of an evil creature possessed the tree when its own physical form was destroyed, imprisoning it within the dried bark and leafless branches.

Local legend says anyone who carves their initials in the tree will take with them a piece of the darkness inside, and it is at the center of many hazing rituals within the Wolf County Community as well as a point of interest for travelers to the area.

Since 1960, almost three hundred people have carved their initials into its bark. In that time, more than one hundred fifty individuals have been found dead within five miles of the tree's base, though the cause of their deaths has never been confirmed. Dozens of others have been reported missing, and, as of 2010, only three cases have resulted in the bodies being found. All three recovered bodies were found hundreds of miles away from the tree, always to the north and among dense forests. The bodies are always found naked and barefoot, with no obvious signs of trauma.

In 2014, the county voted to remove the tree to avoid further incidents, but efforts were stalled due to unknown circumstances.

I think of how Lucas said the Iceheart's spirit needs a human host to survive, how he said the Winter Tree spirit could have been the Iceheart waiting for a victim, and how Shelby said she went somewhere cold but didn't know why.

It almost adds up.

But I have so many more questions.

TWENTY-EIGHT

Shelby's and my drives became awful and our shifts at Nice-N-Spice painfully slow. She didn't speak to customers, though they recognized her. They knew she usually spoke. They knew she usually lit the place up.

She became a storm cloud.

"What is going on with you?" I asked from the passenger seat of her truck. She drove ten miles over the speed limit, and it made my stomach drop each time we hit a curve too fast.

She didn't answer. Instead, she sped up.

I wondered how badly it'd hurt to tuck and roll into the brush at the edge of the road. Would it be worse than dying in an accident when Shelby lost control?

"You have to talk to someone. Come on. I won't even try and fix it, I'll just listen." My fingers gripped the handle above the door for dear life.

More silence.

A crow landed in the center of the road ahead to inspect

the remains of a skunk near the faded yellow line, but hurried back to the safety of a tree at the sight of the Dodge speeding toward it.

"You're going to get fired if the customers keep complaining." It was only half a lie. No customers had complained, at least as far as I knew. But I could see in their eyes that they recognized something dark in my sister, and they didn't trust it.

Shelby let out a heavy breath, then took a turn so fast, my head hit the window.

"What the fuck is wrong with you?" I snapped.

"You're glad Parker stopped inviting me to parties."

"Um, no."

"Of course you are. You were jealous that I had something I liked better than working at this stupid supermarket and hanging out at our crappy house watching movies six months after everyone who already saw them in theaters spoiled the ending."

She swerved a little into the other lane, then righted herself. Her hand shook as she reached for the windshield wipers.

"I had nothing to do with his decision."

"You think I'm out of control just like he does. You all think I might drink too much and do something stupid and draw attention to his stupid parties. He didn't want to get in trouble, but I don't know why you'd care. Let me do what I have to to survive my last months in this shitty town."

"Maybe he's right to think that." How dare she say I have no reason to care about her. "You need help, Shelby."

Shelby seethed over the squeaking of windshield wipers against wet glass.

Freezing rain came down and grayed out the road ahead, but my sister didn't slow. It occurred to me that maybe she didn't care what happened to her, but I didn't want this. I didn't want to die in this truck.

"Can you just slow the fuck down? Do whatever you want, but don't take me out with you."

She slammed on the brakes, and the car behind us laid on the horn as we came to an abrupt stop in the center of the street.

"Is that better?" she says. "Is that fucking better?"

The car behind us passes, and all three of its passengers craned their necks to look at the asshole who almost caused an accident. Shelby's cheeks burned hot and red, and she held the steering wheel in a death grip.

I snatched my backpack off the floor by my feet, and jumped out of the truck before she got moving again. She sped away before I even had the door closed, and a spray of slush drenched me where I stood.

TWENTY-NINE

Charlie stands guard, a slight weight on the bed beside my feet, alert to the sounds of movement outside the door where Shelby is pacing.

Restlessness is a new thing for my sister. At first, she hardly moved, hardly spoke, but tonight during dinner, something changed. It was the first family dinner since she'd come back, and the shift in her tore through us like a storm.

"Shel, please eat your dinner. You need nutrients." All Dad wanted was for her to eat something.

Shelby ignored him, pushing food around her plate. I couldn't help noticing how her skin no longer fit over her bones. The joints in her wrist looked like they belonged to a skeleton twice her size. Her knuckles looked swollen and dark beneath paper-white skin.

My sister has become the image of sickness, but she won't tell us what's wrong.

"Shelby, come on. We're just trying to help you." Mom kept repeating her name, like she's forgotten it. It doesn't feel natural, only necessary.

"You can't." I still hear the way she sounded, another voice layered over hers and echoing her words. "The nightmare isn't over. It is still hungry. It will always be hungry."

"Shelby..." Mom whispered.

"What's hungry?" I asked.

She looked up with rage in her eyes. Her plate of chicken, peas, and buttered noodles hit the wall behind me, barely missing my head. It shattered, pieces of jagged ceramic tumbling to the floor like hail.

It's been almost six hours, and still she paces up and down the hall. She murmurs nonsense loud enough for me to hear through the closed door. *"It is still hungry. It will always be hungry."*

SHELBY'S WORDS repeat through the halls and classrooms of school, through the vacant roads, through the walls of Mel's house. They drain me dry and leave behind the corpse of a girl, hollow and hopeless. I feel nothing. Not the presence of Mel's hand on my shoulder when she asks if I'm okay, not the softness and warmth of the kittens against my skin.

Shelby's getting worse, I text Lucas. Then, I tell him what she repeated as she paced the hall.

Paisley crawls up the sleeve of my sweater, claws tugging at the threads, until she reaches my shoulder where she likes to perch and chew on my hair. Another kitten curls up on my lap against my folded hands. I haven't opened a textbook to study yet. I don't have the energy. For the last hour, I've been letting the cats crawl over me and searching for the comfort and warmth I usually find here.

I don't want to feel like this.

The hands of spirits brush my neck and touch my face. A specter drags its claws up my back, hitting every verte-brae on the way to the base of my skull, where it will seep through my pores and latch onto my brain until I belong to it.

I am not alone.

The presence watches me like it always does, though the kittens haven't noticed yet. I try convincing myself they would. They noticed all the other times, and if there's something here, they'll know.

All four of them have acted normal all afternoon. Well, normal by kitten standards.

But I don't care. Something is wrong.

My phone jabs my ribs from the inner pocket of my jacket. I could text Lucas again. He'd listen. But he also wants me to talk about what I saw in the woods, what I hit with my truck. He'll want to analyze what might be outside today, and I don't want to think about it because the more I do, the more I start bending beneath the weight of Lucas's beliefs.

Paisley hops down from my head and rushes to the windowsill, sudden urgency moving her little legs across the room. Her brother, a solid black kitten, follows her, and the two sit with their noses to the glass and eyes fixed on something in the distance.

The other two hide.

Goosebumps erupt across my body.

The wind shrieks once outside—at least, I think it's the wind—and mimics the dying cry of a wild animal.

The room closes in and the floor sways, no longer solid. No longer safe. Ice crystallizes my blood, and my heart breaks into jagged shards that shred my veins from the inside.

I can't breathe.

Paisley and her brother rush from the windowsill for the safety of hiding.

Something is here.

THIRTY

T reach for my phone and open the camera, then walk to the window.

Staring past the glass, I hold my phone up and hover my thumb over the button to take the picture. I wait for something to appear in the frame. A silhouette. Eyes. Claws. Anything.

Soon, a creature emerges from the trees in the golden dusk, the setting sun illuminating it from behind so it glows. It lifts its head and looks to the window, and I take a photo. Another step closer, another photo.

It stops ten feet from the window and stares at me.

The monster is perfectly still, the desiccated body of a shadow. It stands tall on two legs, limbs stretched to impossible lengths and nothing more than skin over bone.

It wears the skull of another animal over its head, and its familiar eyes burn behind the mask. It doesn't move. Doesn't blink. It doesn't do anything but watch.

So I watch it back, try and rationalize it as a trick, a hoax, a prank.

I can't.

"What do you want?" I ask it. "What do you want from me?"

It doesn't answer, not that I expected it to.

Should I run? Should I shut the lights off and pretend I'm not here? What did Lucas say to do? What did he say about the Iceheart?

I can't remember.

My bones freeze, too heavy now to pull away from this place in front of the window, though I know the glass won't protect me.

The feeling of its eyes on me leaves my skin crawling with thousands of imaginary insects, and I scratch at the feeling.

But I still don't move, don't step back from the window.

I stand there, held hostage by fear and thinking the monster could turn on me at any moment, but it doesn't.

Then, it does the last thing I expect. It turns and lumbers back toward the treeline.

Its withered body moves like even the smallest motions drain what little strength it has. Stick-thin arms dangle at its side, bent slightly at swollen elbows, and claws protrude from the ends of its fingers and add several inches. The light from the chicken coop outlines its figure, drawing my attention to everything wrong with it, from the bulging knee joints to the neck so narrow it shouldn't be able to hold its skull-clad head upright.

How can a creature so slow, so awkward, be such a vicious killer? Maybe it's not what Lucas thought. Yeah. I hold on to that. This thing isn't the Iceheart. It's just... something else.

But if this isn't the Iceheart, how do I begin to comprehend something else even more terrifying?

I slump down against the wall beside the window and

let my trembling hands fall to the floor. The phone tumbles from my fingers and onto the carpet beside me.

It may be gone now, but the monster can return anytime.

I need to warn Mel, so I text her and tell her I saw the coyote again.

Then I text Lucas. *There was something here.*

With shaking thumbs mispelling words, I send another message seconds later begging him to come to Mel's so I can talk to him.

Each time I press send, my hands begin drafting another message. My mind races, spewing words onto the screen with either the wrong letters or the right ones out of order. He has to answer. He can't be busy.

I need him.

I don't even care right now that I hate that I need him.

Lead weight pulls me down until I lie on my side, phone cradled in my hand. I stay there until Paisley emerges from her hiding place and returns to me. She curls up between my arm and my chest and dozes off, but I still don't feel safe.

Be there in 15. Don't move.

My body feels so ragged, I don't think I could move if I wanted to.

I scroll through the pictures I took of the monster, though my eyes won't focus and they're all blurry anyway. Even the best one has the monster soft around edges I know are sharp, and its horrid eyes smear from how my hands shook. My head spins as I try to focus, and I set my phone facedown beside me to block the light.

Time stands still. Fifteen minutes pass like mud, thick seconds that tug at me like a vicious current. They creep into my lungs, achingly heavy, and force out the breath I need to survive.

Lucas may only be coming for the information I have, but I don't care. We aren't friends—neither of us has fallen for that illusion—but I have no choice now but to trust him to help me with this.

When his knock comes on the front door, I tear a breath of air into my lungs. I text him first to be sure the monster hasn't returned. *Is that you?*

I'm here.

Paisley grumbles when I move, and I cradle her in one arm when I go to the door. In the glow of headlights, Lucas breathes into his hands to warm them. The night is clear but sharp, and the cold cuts into me in the short time I have the door open to let Lucas in.

"Hey," he says. "Are you okay?"

"It... was here. I think..." I scratch between Paisley's ears for comfort that doesn't come. "I think it came for me."

He nods a few times and sticks his hands in his pockets.

"Do you think you'd mind driving me home?" he asks as he closes the door behind him. "My mom said she'd come, but she shouldn't be driving in the dark. Her vision's never been good at night."

"Why couldn't you just take the car?" The question comes out harsher than I mean, but I go with it. It gives me something to fixate on instead of the thing I saw earlier.

"I don't drive."

"Don't you think that's important, considering you're apparently the only person in town who can deal with this stuff?"

He frowns, carving deep lines around his mouth, and casts his eyes to my feet.

"I haven't been able to take driver's ed yet. Not much money in monster hunting, and most of what we make goes toward paying the bills." He shifts on his feet, awkward. "She usually doesn't mind driving. She misses it, the work. Her accident meant she had to retire before she was ready."

Now I feel like an asshole. I shouldn't have said anything. I should know people simply can't afford to drive, or they prioritize differently. He and I have that in common, and it helps me understand him a bit more.

"I'm sorry."

"It is what it is."

We sit on the ground in the kittens' room, and Paisley abandons my lap in favor of this new person. Traitor. He holds his hands up, palms out, and goes rigid like he doesn't know what to do with her. Apparently he only knows how to handle the big, scary monsters of the world.

"She won't hurt you. Well... she does bite, actually."

His face goes pale, and he looks down at the oblivious kitten kneading the fabric of his pants.

"You good?" I ask.

He doesn't respond except to stare at Paisley. "When I was little, I was attacked by a stray. It was probably my fault but I don't... don't really like being near cats."

I pluck Paisley off his lap and hold her in mine despite her protests. Then I shift the conversation in another direction, despite my instinct to sink my teeth deeper into his fear. "So," I begin. "How do you explain this?"

Lucas accepts my phone when I hand it to him, photo open on the screen. His jaw drops as he zooms in for a better look.

"I can't believe you got this," he says. "The hunters have

depended on sketches for this thing as long as we've known it existed."

"That's it then? That's the Iceheart?" He nods, and I keep talking. "It wasn't very fast, and it didn't seem like it gave a shit about attacking me."

Lucas continues looking at the photo.

"And how do you explain the animal skull? How does it feed with it on?"

"I... it doesn't feed. Can't. Not with the skull..." he trails off, then digs his laptop out of his bag. "I've heard of this. Or, it sounds familiar."

His fingers fly across the keyboard as he looks for answers to my question. From where I sit, I only make out some of the words on the screen, enough to know I don't have a good feeling.

"Here." He points to an image on the computer. It's a rough sketch of a thin creature wearing a skull like I saw earlier. "The exact species hasn't been identified here, but there were reports in the early nineties of a tall, emaciated monster wearing a mask a couple hours north of here."

"Why would it do that?"

"Some carnivorous shifters like the Iceheart have been observed doing similar things. While the host has strength, they can create a sort of muzzle to prevent the spirit from feeding. When they shift into the monster's true form, their body grows and conforms to the inside of the skull. The mask prevents the monster from opening its jaw."

"What?" I heard and processed every word he said, but I need him to say it again.

He does.

"That is, literally, the worst thing I have ever heard." I stroke Paisley's fur to distract myself from talk of shapeshifters, muzzles, feeding, everything.

I'm too tired to fight off the image of someone putting on a skull to stop themselves from cannibalizing another person. My stomach twists as my imagination takes the idea and runs with it, forcing in the thought of someone stretching out to something twice their size and feeling the bones of another creature closing around their skull.

"The claws—" I point at the screen. "I know those claws."

"It's what you saw in the woods the other night."

An explanation should make me feel better, especially one I've seen with my own eyes and captured in an image to prove I'm not losing my mind.

"You hit it with your truck. That's what made those marks."

"I know." I guess I always did. There was no better explanation. The ones I made up were riddled with holes and inconsistencies. It never mattered that I didn't want this to be real. "How do I keep it away? Can I?"

"Fire. Keep a candle lit. Even the slightest heat will keep it far enough away."

A candle. Easy. Mom must have some old ones she never burned hidden in the back of the closet. She won't notice if I take them.

"Okay," I say.

Lucas's left foot taps and makes his knee bounce. It distracts me and makes me nervous, and I want to put my hand out to stop it from moving so rapidly. I don't.

"Why are you helping me?" I ask. "I've been awful to you this whole time. Longer than that."

He breathes out, a heavy exhale, and leans forward with his elbows on his knees. With him staring straight forward, I can't see his eyes. I only see the way the corner of his mouth twitches with every moment he lets pass without an answer.

"This territory is my responsibility, as the only remaining Powell able to do the job. I have to protect this place."

THIRTY-ONE

Charlie wakes me from nightmares of the monster, and I try to nudge her off my bed so I can get back to sleep. I don't know how long it's been since the last time I got a restful night, but it doesn't look like tonight will be successful. The cat digs her claws into the sheets and growls as I push her.

Her eyes glisten in the light of the candle lit beside my bed, pupils wide as the moon. Her body is tense, alert.

The creaky screen door slams shut and echoes through the house, and I curse myself for forgetting to take it down before winter came.

I check the time on my phone. Three twenty-six. Dad wouldn't be home this early, and I heard Mom go to bed hours ago. It leaves only one other possibility. Shelby being the source of the noise would explain the cat's agitation. The two have no interest in getting along.

Charlie darts beneath my bed when I open my bedroom door, and I step out into the hall with a fleece blanket wrapped tight around my shoulders.

The outside light by the front door throws strange

shapes through the windows of the kitchen and they creep into the hallway. The glow extends the shadows of chair spindles into wretched fingers reaching for me, the oval glass insert in the door becomes a gaping maw ready to swallow everything within reach. My own house, the only home I've ever known, becomes a monster in itself, and I wish I could turn around, unsee these things, and go back to bed.

But I'd only lie awake awaiting my alarm, fighting the icy tendrils of winter that creep in through the old window. They dance up my skin, ignoring the blanket wrapped around me, and freeze me from the outside in.

"Hello?" I say into the dark. "Shelby?"

My pulse riots in my throat as I reach for the light switch in the kitchen.

"What are you doing?" Shelby resembles a raccoon caught rummaging through the trash as she fills a glass with water from the sink.

"Interesting question. What are *you* doing? Where were you?"

She wears rumpled jeans with a few inches of melted snow around the bottom and a long-sleeved T-shirt. Her hair looks like she's been sleeping on it, but the light in the room betrays the presence of a twig.

"Have you been in the woods?" I ask.

She doesn't have any socks or shoes on.

"I felt like going for a walk."

"Barefoot? In February? Where are your shoes, Shel?"

She takes a sip from her water, but her arm is rigid like she doesn't really want to drink it. She taps a bare foot in an uneven rhythm on the linoleum floor, and the nervous movement makes me uncomfortable.

"It wasn't long," she says. "Just a minute."

I narrow my eyes.

"Why are you acting like this?" I'm sick of excusing everything she does. Her behavior doesn't make sense. *She* doesn't make sense, and every day it gets worse.

"This is me now."

"What happened to you?" I'm so sick of asking the same questions.

She dumps the rest of her water into the sink and rinses the glass like a single-minded robot.

"Being gone emptied me out. There's nothing left of me, and nothing will fix that."

Instead of her usual dry tone or the creepy layered voice from the other night, a glimmer of emotion sneaks into her words. The confession destroys what little remains of her, like she has to accept her secrets as her own before she can share them with the rest of us.

"I wanted to get out of here but I should have said goodbye." She hugs her arms to her chest. "But now I've been gone so long, all the good parts of me are lost. I thought it would be better if you thought I was dead, but it took me here. It made me come. I didn't want to do this to you and Mom and Dad."

I reach for her, but she pulls away. Her story contradicts the things she said when she first came back. Was she lying then, or is she lying now?

"But you said... you said you wanted to see us. I thought you wanted to come back?"

She meets my gaze, eyes rimmed with glistening tears. "It makes me say things I don't mean. I can't fight it anymore. This might be the last time we talk before it takes over completely."

I clutch the edges of my blanket tighter around my body to hide the ambush of goosebumps over my skin.

"It uses me to blend in. It brought me here, to its hunting grounds, and it is so, so hungry."

It is still hungry. It will always be hungry.

"Is that what happened to the girl in the woods?"

"Yes, and she won't be the only one."

"If you know something, please tell me. You have to help us stop this. Don't you want to help?" I plead.

"I can't. You won't understand." Her mood shifts, and she blinks away her tears. She looks at me with a storm in her eyes. "You won't forgive me for what I've done."

"It doesn't matter what you've done. Do something now. Earn your forgiveness, if that's what you want."

"I can't stay here. It isn't safe for you."

My sister doesn't make any sense. First she says she has no control, then she says she's going to leave. I can't tell which pieces of the story are true anymore. Maybe I never could.

"I thought it wouldn't let you." I say.

She shakes her head.

"You have to tell Mom and Dad. You can't leave them without saying goodbye."

She says nothing. No apology, no affirmation that she won't disappear without a word.

"I'll tell them everything. I kept too many secrets for you, and maybe if I'd told them sooner, this wouldn't be happening. I'm not lying anymore." I try to sound intimidating, threatening, but I can't muster it. I sound small, hopeless.

"They won't believe you."

"Then I'll tell the hunters."

This time, the threat lands. She freezes for a fraction of a second, a deer caught in headlights.

Then my sister walks past me without glancing back in

my direction, and I let her go. There is nothing left of her, nothing for me to try and save. She is an unrecognizable version of my sister who walks around wearing Shelby's face. The way she talks, the way she stands, all of it is wrong.

Once I hear her door close, I pull a pair of boots on over my socks and step outside into the flickering light. It has gotten dimmer, but still illuminates the night enough for me to see the path away from the door.

I close the screen gently behind me and search the half inch of fluffy snow for footprints. The February air gnaws on my bones as I stand there wrapped in my blanket, scanning every inch of snow until I find what I came here for. A trail of footprints, the right size to belong to Shelby and made by bare feet, leads to the front door, but not from the driveway where a car would've dropped her off. No, her footprints lead home from the forest.

THIRTY-TWO

I sit on the floor in the kittens' room, losing a battle to keep my eyelids open and replaying Shelby's and my conversation from last night. Lucas sits against the wall across from me, focused on the computer he brought for our "research project." That's what I told Mel when I asked if he could come along. A research project. I guess it isn't technically a lie.

"You okay?" Lucas asks.

"Yeah. Sure." I may be done lying for Shelby, but I can still lie to preserve myself. "I talked to Shelby last night. It was awful."

"What did you talk about?" He speaks carefully, measured.

I tell him the parts that stand out most, with all their contradictions and inconsistencies. I tell him she's going to try and leave again.

"I told her I would tell the hunters, and she got weird. Like she didn't expect me to know about you."

"We've encountered the Iceheart before, so it's possible it remembers us," Lucas says.

157

"That makes sense, but why would Shelby know? Could it, I don't know, tell her about you? To watch out for you?"

"I don't know."

I lean my head back against the wall, too tired to ask more questions. Exhaustion pushes my senses into overdrive. The daylight burns my eyes, even when I pull the shades down to cast the room in shadow. The slightest sound deafens me. Lucas's fingers clicking against the computer keyboard becomes torture. The cats' purring thunders in my ears.

And all I can smell is trash.

Rotten, hot trash like a bag left outside on the stickiest summer day. It smells almost sweet in its decay, like fruits decomposing in the open for everyone to draw in with their breaths. It suffocates me. I want to be sick.

My stomach turns, and I gag.

"Do you smell that?" I whisper when Lucas looks my way.

"What?" He searches for the scent. "I don't smell anything."

I cover my mouth and nose with the neck of my sweater. "The garbage? You don't smell the garbage?"

He shakes his head, and I rise to look for messes the cats could have made. The litterboxes are clean, and they haven't vomited in any of their usual places.

"Maybe Mel forgot to take the trash out," I mutter, already halfway out the door.

Despite the fact that I know Mel wouldn't leave trash long enough to fester like this, I go into the kitchen and check. As expected, the trashcan contains a mostly fresh bag with only a spent filter of coffee grounds tossed inside. I check the fridge, the cupboards, anywhere food could have spoiled unnoticed. Nothing.

The smell persists to the point where I go outside and check the big bins, even though it's too cold for them to be the source of it.

"What's going on?" Lucas asks when I return.

"I don't know. Nothing."

"You should rest. I'll sit with the cats if you need sleep." His shoulders tense. He doesn't want to be alone with the cats, but he insists. "I'll wake you up if anything weird happens."

I slump against the wall. "I can't sleep." Not with this smell weaving its way through the creases in my brain.

"You should try," he says.

"Why? I'm just tired. People get tired all the time. They get through it. I will too."

He crosses his arms and his expression becomes serious. "You can't be weak. It'll give the Iceheart the advantage if it decides to lure you in."

"Fine," I groan.

I stomp to the bathroom where Mel keeps a bottle of Benadryl, and take two hoping they'll knock me out. Then I take one of the fleece blankets from a basket in the kitten room and make myself comfortable on the floor with my jacket as a pillow. The blanket almost thaws the newly arrived cold in my fingertips.

Two kittens come and curl up against my stomach, and the weight of their bodies almost equals that of Charlie. They radiate warmth, and their purring calms my nerves. Eventually, my thoughts go quiet and my muscles relax. For the first time in more than a week, I slip into unconsciousness despite the smell of trash still lingering in my nostrils.

❄

THERE'S a scream in my throat when I wake.

I don't recognize this place.

I push myself up with hands slippery from sweat. They slide against the smooth leather of a couch I don't recall falling asleep on. Darkness fills the room around me except for the glow of a light from beneath a closed door.

As my eyes adjust, I find shadows surrounding me.

Monsters. Dozens of them in all different sizes, bloody eyes all locked on me. Bright red, angry eyes that could only belong to a demon, a beast from the lowest depths of hell.

They circle in closer, chanting a language I don't speak.

I'm so hot. Is something burning nearby? Sweat drenches the fabric of my clothes so they cling to my body. The heat of a fever devours me.

"Go away." I croak the words. My throat feels dry as sandpaper, and my tongue is no better. "Go away," I say again.

One of them reaches for me with long fingers comprised of inches of claw grown through gray-skinned tips. It drags against my arm, leaving a trail of ice along my skin.

The scream breaks free.

"Cara? What's wrong?" A hollow, distant voice asks.

Where am I? Who is here with me?

The voice disturbs the monsters. They disappear like they were never there at all. With them gone, I am alone. The voice I heard belongs to no one.

The heat drives me mad, and I peel off my sweater and toss it aside. I tangle in my T-shirt, too damp from my fever, and give up on tearing it off too. My boots come next, then my socks.

Too hot. Too hot. Too *hot*.

"What are you doing?" The voice comes again.

I throw aside my blanket in the direction of the voice

and stand, surrounded by monsters again. One of them stands taller and clearer than all the others, as if the rest are only copies of it, and reaches out again with another of those sickening hands. The horde mirrors the gesture, a thousand fingers reaching for me. Beckoning.

I whip my body away and run to a door on the opposite side of the room.

The monsters follow, and I rush out into the forest. The air feels stale on my skin as I boil from heat deep in my marrow.

I weave through trees that warp into daggers around me. Branches like talons grab at me, and I dodge their attempts at closing around my ankles, my waist, anything they can get a hold of.

Get away. Get away. Get away.

My heart slams against my ribs and my leg muscles scream in protest as I run. Both my lungs shrivel and die in my chest, rejecting the oxygen I drag in. The forest floor shreds the soles of my bare feet, but adrenaline dulls the pain. It dulls everything.

The monsters are still behind me.

The stench of rot still follows me, and I gag between wasted breaths. My stomach heaves acid up my throat, but I swallow it down. Tears prick the corners of my eyes with the sting of the bile, and sourness coats my tongue.

I can't breathe.

Panic consumes me. The forest shows its hostility, with monsters waiting in every copse of trees and hungry whispers from every direction.

In the distance, a shriek fractures the entire world, and I cover my ears with my hands as if they can protect me. The creature screams again, agony lacing the violence of its cry.

A tree catches me off guard and hooks my foot with an

elevated root. I fly forward for eternity, then land hard on my right shoulder. I tumble down a hill and crash through a tiny iced-over stream. My bones meet rocks and more roots, and pain sears every inch of my body. Then my skull hits something and my vision splits in two for the moment before everything goes dark.

THIRTY-THREE

I had the worst case of cramps ever experienced by humanity, and Shelby was in the bathroom getting ready for a party she was uninvited to. Because of course she was.

My abdomen screamed for the painkillers on the other side of the locked door, and my entire body broke into a sweat. I would rather avoid her, but the agony was worse than any damage she could do.

"I'm in here," she said, annoyed. They were the first three words she'd said to me since leaving me to walk to Nice-N-Spice.

"No shit. Can you get out?"

"Wait your turn." There was no playfulness in her demand, only ice.

I stomped away—well, in spirit I did—and went to my room for one of the bobby pins piled on my desk. Two could play her game. I learned how to be an asshole from the very best, after all.

The bathroom fan hummed unevenly as I jammed the pin into the tiny hole on the doorknob. The lock popped, and I threw my weight into storming the tiny room.

"Fuck, Cara." Shelby slammed her fist on the edge of the sink.

I pushed her out of the way and grabbed the plastic bottle of pills from the medicine cabinet.

On my way out, I glared at her. Even with layers of makeup, she looked sick. The pale pink blush she brushed on her cheeks looked fake, and, if she'd used concealer, it wasn't doing enough to hide the bluish-black circles beneath her eyes.

"You shouldn't go to that party." A wasted breath, really.

She narrowed her eyes at me, then shoved me out of the bathroom. I stood there for a minute, considering barging back in and making her talk to me, but I didn't have the energy. My legs felt like Jell-O, if Jell-O was made from lead instead of sugar.

"I'm not going to lie for you," I said as I leaned against the wall. "I'll tell Mom you're at a party."

No response.

"She'll ground you. Then you'll be stuck here."

All I had were empty threats. Mom had no power over Shelby. Nobody did.

She had nothing to say to me, so I retreated to my room where I wrapped myself in blankets and tried to ignore the stabbing pain in my abdomen while the pills did their work. Eventually, I dozed off a little until Shelby left and slammed the front door. Her truck's tires squealed as she tore out of the driveway.

"Where's your sister?" Mom asked when she came home from the electronics shop.

"She's at Emily's watching old Stephen King movies," I lied. I didn't want to lie for her, but I was too afraid of what my sister might do if I told the truth.

THIRTY-FOUR

I wake in a clearing, swallowed by midnight's darkness.

Skeleton trees loom over me from all sides, leafless branches reaching for my body. Their roots cradle me where I lay, presenting my body like a sacrifice to whatever brought me out here.

My head aches like nothing I've felt before, and my vision doubles so the forest looks thicker.

There are no monsters here.

Or they are hiding.

Stillness and silence crawl in like insects through my ears, and I would scream if not for the fact that my throat refuses. I can't speak or swallow or even clear the blockage behind my tongue.

The smell from earlier fills my nostrils. The smell of decay.

God, maybe it's me.

I search the clearing for anything else that could be the source of the scent, but a blanket of snow covers everything. Any decomposing things would require digging to find, and the cold would preserve them until the spring thaw.

A sound comes from the other side of the clearing. A low growl. I turn in its direction and find several pairs of yellow eyes lurking in the brush—coyotes and foxes, raccoons and fishers. Hungry things that haven't had a good meal for a long time.

I force away the thought of being the next pile of bones someone finds in these woods.

The growling intensifies, and another creature adds its voice—a bloodcurdling screech—to the chorus. I hold up my hands, not that the skinny things will do anything against the sharp teeth of an animal whose entire life depends on being able to use them.

I rise from where I lie among the roots and look down to find snow filling the space between my toes. Had I not looked, I wouldn't have noticed the bareness of my feet.

The temperature should have killed me by now, but I feel nothing. Comfortable, even.

What is happening to me?

The bare flesh of my arms doesn't even have goosebumps, though this is still February and I am still in Minnesota. At some point, I tossed aside my jacket and sweater. I don't remember doing that. I only remember the monsters.

Why am I alive? How?

Am I dead? A ghost? For all I know, the monsters already tore me apart and discarded the useless pieces.

The animals go quiet, and I look for the eyes again. They still lurk within the bushes, watching me. I feel it.

Finally, the pair of eyes I've been expecting emerges from the shadows. I know them all too well now, but don't understand why they're here.

An image flashes in my head, so violently it knocks me back to the ground. A cabin out in the woods, covered in snow except for a path shoveled from the door to a pile of firewood under a tarp. The corner of the blue plastic sheet blows in the breeze, exposing some of the split wood. Two rocking chairs sit at the porch, both worn from years of use and weather. The porch, the whole cabin, really, doesn't look much better.

Then it vanishes and I'm back in the forest.

The monster steps closer to me, out of the brush and into the clearing. I can't move. I mean to, but I can't.

The cabin returns, like I'm there and not in the middle of the woods. The vision drags me inside, where I find the remains of hunting clothes drenched in blood. Pieces of bone like shards of ceramic form islands in the dark pools of red on the wooden floor.

Footprints, animal and human, lead away from the gore, and I follow them with my gaze.

Before I see who they lead to, the scene ends. I return to the forest.

A voice echoes in my head. A girl's voice—not the monster, but not quite familiar either. *Please go. I didn't want you to see this. I don't want to hurt you.*

Please.

Please go.

The cabin, the bodies, the blood flicker behind my eyes once more before I focus on the sight before me. The monster stands flanked on either side by a group of predators—not just coyotes and foxes and bobcats, but wolves. Wolves long banished from this part of the world. Hungry birds wait in trees, craving the taste of their prey.

They stare at me, unmoving until the monster gives the command. It watches without its skull mask, and I watch back. Its red eyes spill down its face in a way I thought had been a trick of the light before. But no, a blurry uneven glow hovers around them like its body hadn't planned on needing eye sockets, so it clawed out the openings itself.

I take a step back.

This thing is a nightmare.

Tired, gray skin pulls tight over a too-big skeleton to the point of splitting at the elbows and knees. Dried blood covers those spots, healing into stiff scars over stained bones. Jagged, torn skin hangs over its mouth, as if it chewed through its lips to satiate its hunger. Serrated teeth of mismatched sizes glisten with blood.

It glares at me. Sizes me up.

It lifts a leg, joints creaking with the slow effort of movement, to come closer. Its pack follows. Mere inches from me now, I smell the death on it. I've been smelling the slow decay of its body as it wastes away. Rancid, sour flesh stings my nostrils, and I heave hot bile onto the snow.

The Iceheart unlocks its jaw and lowers those teeth to my level, frigid breath hitting my face. I am its victim today. Tomorrow, someone will report me missing, but I won't be found. The monster and its pack will ravage my body, my bones, and let the snow keep what little remains.

The animals pace, eager to sink their teeth into me. The monster denies them their feast. They may eat when the Iceheart is finished.

I close my eyes, hold my breath, and wait for pain to set in when my skin tears beneath the pressure of teeth. But it never comes. A violent heat comes in the place of fear, of delirium, or everything that made me run into this forest, and my mind suddenly clears.

I feel nothing.

When I open my eyes, the monster's pack has turned

away to retreat back into the dark. The Iceheart still leans forward, burning the memory of its face into my memory for life.

A whisper rides in the wind around me. This time, I recognize the voice.

I didn't want you to see me like this. I don't want to hurt you.

I don't want to hurt you.

I don't want to.

THIRTY-FIVE

The Iceheart lets me go.

So I run.

I weave through the trees, eyes adjusting to the dark well enough to dodge errant branches or push them away with my hands. Lower bushes snap against my ankles and shins, tear my jeans, and cut thin lines in my skin.

The moon outlines the trees like ghosts, and they follow me. They won't let me leave here alive. They want me to stay, to become part of them.

But the Iceheart let me go, and I will not let the forest take me.

A cry for help lingers in my throat, a swarm of vibrations afraid to be free in the world. There is no help. There is no one.

My head aches and I don't know whether the fall or the Iceheart being in my head caused it. That's what that vision was. It wanted me to see that cabin, to see what it could do to me if it chose to.

I don't understand why it didn't.

There are no markers on the trees because nobody maintains trails out here. Dry brush grows in tangles over a path made by wildlife. Not a soul has been out here in a while, not even the animals that used this path to search for food. All I can hope is that I find a road passing through the wilderness.

The cloudiness of confusion has cleared a little, and I piece together the events leading up to me being here. I was at Mel's, and Lucas was there too. I took a nap—but don't remember waking up. Could this be a nightmare I haven't woken from? How do I get out if it is?

The image of the cabin returns to me, featureless hunters replaced with Lucas on the floor. The fear stops me from running and forces me to catch my breath. Did the monster take him too?

My feet leave behind bloody footprints in the snow, torn from the forest floor, but I keep going. I'll walk until I find safety, or I'll walk until I die.

I haven't decided which it will be.

I lose my footing on uneven ground and tumble a few feet down a small hill. The same shoulder I landed on earlier breaks my fall at the bottom, and a wave of dull pain travels through me.

For a while, I stay there, sinking in the snow. I can't rest, but I don't have the strength to push myself up.

I lift my head and search for signs of the Iceheart. Maybe it let me go as a game, so it can wear me out before it finally kills me. Is that how it hunts? I don't remember what Lucas said. I think he mentioned something about hunting behavior.

Damn it, why can't I remember anything?

I didn't want you to see me like this. I don't want to hurt you.

I remember the voice that appeared in my head when the Iceheart showed me the cabin.

I don't want to hurt you.

It's playing with me. Showing me murders. Planting my sister's voice in my mind like a song buffering on too slow internet.

Please go.

The Iceheart wants to turn me against her. Or try to. She escaped and it wants to make her the monster. That has to be what she's so afraid of, being seen as a killer. The kind with nothing to stop her from tearing her victims apart like they were never human to begin with.

Please.

I don't know how to help her. I need to make it back to Lucas. He'll know what to do.

He has to prove she didn't do this.

Ahead, the trees thin and a vehicle has packed the snow down—an ATV maybe. The discovery lends me the energy to move a little faster. This could be good.

The boost of energy doesn't last long. I've been out here forever. I could have walked clear over the Canadian border without noticing. The forest is unceremonious about things like that.

Pain in the bottom of my feet starts to break through the numbness and shoot up my leg. The sharpness tells me I'm not dreaming. I'm really here.

At the end of the vehicle tracks, I come to another clearing. It stops me midstep, and my hand covers my mouth in horror.

The sight of a cabin—the exact one the Iceheart showed me—makes my knees weak and I fall to the snow.

THIRTY-SIX

The only difference between what the Iceheart showed me and the cabin before me is a shed to one side, door swinging open, with two red ATVs parked side by side. I could take one, if I wanted—and I do —but the cabin draws me to it instead. Curiosity forces me to knock once on the front door, which creaks open a bit before I turn the handle. Someone has been here recently. They forgot to lock up.

Heat from inside pummels me along with the smell of a burnt-out fire. A few logs are scattered across the ground, dropped before they could be ignited. Beads of sweat collect behind my knees and around my neck where the collar meets skin, so I leave the door open for the cold to follow.

I don't call out as I go deeper into the room. Instead I leave blood on the floor as I creep around to find a phone. That's what I tell myself, at least.

But I know what I came here for moments before I find the remains. Two bodies—well, I really can't call them bodies when all that's left are bits of bone—lay in a pile on the floor. Shreds of winter camouflage soak up the little pools of blood, still wet and deep red. To one side, a boot has been discarded with crusted, rust-colored stains on the leather.

Two skulls sit intact, emptied of edible parts and tossed aside, and I stare at them. The sockets no longer house the eyes, but still they stare at me. I should have done something to stop this.

The metallic stench of blood lingers in the air, still fresh, still warm.

Bile burns its way up my throat and onto the floor beside the blood. I catch my balance with a hand on the arm of a tacky Christmas plaid sofa, though my arm trembles beneath my own weight. I know this place. Do I know the people scattered across the floor?

I can't look at the mess now that I remember the cabin —Parker's family's cabin. Shelby's ex-boyfriend. Another victim of this forest.

My heart skips as it pounds in my throat. I need to get out of here.

Footprints meander toward the door, unrecognizable at first and then human near the end.

A rifle lays beside the blood. I take it, hug it close to my chest, then look around the cabin for a phone, a computer, anything I can use to call for help. I find a cell phone on the counter, the kind that flips open to expose a little screen and keyboard. It has barely enough battery to make a call and only a single bar of reception, but I try anyway.

I get through to the dispatcher. Tell him where I am. What I've found.

He says something back to me, but I can't focus. It's too hot and I keep remembering things I wanted to bury.

Shelby perched on the arm of that horrendous sofa with a drink in one hand and a drunken grin on her face. Shelby leaning against the counter in the kitchen and telling Parker how much vodka to put in her vodka cranberry. Shelby throwing darts at a board on the wall and missing every time.

I pinch my eyes shut.

"Ma'am, are you still there?" the dispatcher asks.

"What?"

The dispatcher repeats the question again, but I can't focus. I can't breathe in the heat of this cabin. Can't stop thinking about Shelby.

Why is the Iceheart doing this? Torturing me with memories of my sister? I'd rather it just kill me.

"Is there any identification on the bodies?"

"No. There's nothing left."

"Surely there's some—"

I cut him off. "I said there's nothing left." My voice shakes, betraying fear and exhaustion and all the things I feel right now.

"Okay. Okay, calm down."

I snap. "Don't tell me to calm down. Would you be calm right now? No. Get me out of here." The syllables break, fray at the edges. "I don't want to die."

The faint sound of typing comes from the other end before he dares to say anything else. My breath falls heavy on the mouthpiece of the phone, but I wait. I try to be patient while death surrounds me.

Outside, the wind howls—at least, I hope it's the wind and not the Iceheart coming back for me.

The dispatcher asks another question. Well, he tries to, but the phone cuts him off as it dies in my hand.

THIRTY-SEVEN

The monster haunts me, appearing every time I close my eyes. Its teeth gnaw through the skin around its mouth, glimmering with blood and bits of torn flesh. Between visions of the Iceheart, I catch flickers of the cabin around me. More memories from the few parties I went to with Shelby.

How long have I been here?

Where are the police?

I imagine the monster burying those teeth like daggers into the bodies of the hunters I found. Riotous screams burst from their throats and shred their vocal cords until the sounds croak and break apart like the static of a dying radio broadcast. Sticky, crimson liquid bubbles up around the monster's cheeks, smears across its face, and spills onto the floor in a puddle.

"Miss? Are you okay?" a voice asks, soft and comforting but so far away.

A hand touches my shoulder, and I flinch from the heat on my skin.

"It's all right," they say. "We're here to help you."

I can't focus. Fever consumes me, turns my bones to ashes. Delirium clutches at me with claws dug deep into the sides of my skull.

The police are here, but they may as well be ghosts.

Monsters watch from the shadows, but the police don't notice. How do they not see them? Miniature Icehearts lick blood off their faces with unnaturally long tongues. Some hold bones, digging out the marrow, picking at bits of flesh. Others simply wait, patiently, for their next victim.

Strong arms lift me from where I sit on the ground. Everything goes black, dead quiet. I no longer hear the sounds of the feast.

"We're taking you to the hospital." The faraway voice returns. "You're going to be okay."

I think I argue with them, but I can't be sure.

Sweat drowns me. My soaked T-shirt clings to my body, and I've torn the collar to shreds. Another layer—a blanket? Someone's coat?—hangs over my shoulders, and I roast.

The fabric wraps around me, choking me with its warmth, and I toss it aside.

"You're going to freeze out there dressed like this," the faraway voice says.

"I don't want it. It's too hot."

The cabin passes in a blur as I float to the door. People dressed in blue fill the room, investigating. They spin around and around. They split in two, then four, then eight. There are so many of them.

Someone carries me into a loud vehicle, and hot hands touch my neck, my wrist, my forehead. Gentle hands inspect my ruined feet. The sharp relief of cold metal clicks around one wrist.

Doors slam.

People talk.

The vehicle moves, spins the whole world. There's nothing left for me to vomit, but I retch until tears stream down my face.

I pinch my eyes shut against the voice in my head. It isn't really Shelby. It sounds like her, but it's a trick, a game designed to break me.

"The heat is miserable, isn't it?" the Iceheart asks in my sister's voice.

Shelby said something like that before. What was it? It was like drowning. She's right about that.

"What are you doing to me?"

Fake-Shelby laughs.

Someone else answers.

"We don't know," they say. "Once we make sure you're okay, we'll have some questions for you, so we can figure out what happened out here."

I don't answer them. My question wasn't for them.

"Leave me alone," I plead to the blur at the edge of my vision, deadly red and hungry. "Leave me alone. Leave me alone. *Leave me alone.*"

I thrash against straps holding me down. Over and over, I scream for it to leave me alone.

The blur flickers.

Dies, then reanimates.

I blink it away again, and the rest of the universe tips sideways.

THIRTY-EIGHT

Shelby didn't go to school. She left the keys to the truck on the counter with a note that said she wasn't feeling well. I figured she had a hangover when she snuck into the house in the middle of the night after Parker's party, but after finding the note, I wasn't so sure.

"Cara," someone called out behind me as I swapped books in my locker. Emily. She looked awful.

"Hey," I said. "Shelby's home sick today."

Because of course Emily didn't really want to talk to me. She was Shelby's friend, not mine.

"I figured." Emily's eyes were rimmed red and bloodshot.

"What do you mean?" Shelby might not tell me anything, but Emily would. Emily wasn't the type to keep secrets, at least not the juicy kind.

"She didn't tell you?"

I shook my head.

"She just said she was sick," I said. "Via sticky note. So, no."

Emily frowned. Looked around. Leaned in closer. "Parker died."

"What? How? When?"

"Sometime between the party and yesterday morning. He"—her eyes welled up with tears—"He was talking to Shelby, and he was so drunk. They had a fight. Right there in front of everyone, and then she left. I don't even know if she was drinking, but I couldn't get to her in time and she left."

Emily heaved desperate breaths between each word until she lost control of herself. I didn't want to hug her, but I did and she cried into my shoulder.

"Parker went after her. His friends tried to stop him but he still left."

"Did he... did he get in an accident?" I asked.

"No. I mean, maybe? But not in his car. We found it stalled out halfway down the driveway. You know how it's like eight miles long, right? It was just there, battery dead and everything."

Emily sobbed again, and the violence of it shook me to my core.

"They found him yesterday afternoon. The cops. The dogs from the county sniffed him out."

"Emily..." I said, breathless. I needed to know, but at the same time I didn't want to.

"Something ate him."

"How do you know?" It was a stupid question. Everyone knew Emily's cousin was a deputy.

She looked up at me, not daring to say who told her how Parker was found.

"I'm sorry," I said. What else could I do?

Emily wiped her nose on the sleeve of her coat and straightened her posture. "Can you text me and let me know Shelby's okay? Please?"

I nodded, and pulled out my phone, added her number to my contacts. Then I opened a text to my sister. How could she not tell me Parker was dead? Did she even know?

Hey, I'm sorry about Parker. I typed the message, then deleted it. She might not know.

I typed a dozen more before I finally settled on something that wasn't too alarming.

Hey, we should talk.

She responded in a second.

There's nothing to talk about.

THIRTY-NINE

"Why were you in the cabin, Cara?" the faraway voice asks.

We aren't moving anymore. The blurred monster is gone. A metal chair holds my weight and I sit upright beneath a blinding lamp.

I tug at the sleeves of a sweater I don't recall putting on. The temperature commands my attention, a dull burn on the surface of my skin.

"I don't know," I say. "I thought you were bringing me to the hospital."

"You were there for two days. They discharged you yesterday."

Mentally, I count the days from when I think I went into the woods. It should be Sunday, or maybe Monday. My heart seizes.

"I missed work," I whisper. "Did someone call my boss for me?"

"You have other things to worry about."

The room straightens out, and I find the soft edges of a white woman dressed in a deputy's uniform. She sits across from me, arms folded on the table. I wish I could read her expression, but her features blend together.

"You understand how this looks for you, right? Having been at two separate scenes of suspicious deaths with no good explanation."

They can't possibly think I killed those people.

"I can't help you if you don't tell me why you were out there," she says.

"Can't we postpone this interrogation until she's feeling better?" Dad speaks up from somewhere nearby. Is he next to me? The figures on either side of me have no features either. "She's still recovering from a concussion."

"If Cara wants to talk at another time, we can."

"No, I'll talk now." The sooner I get out of here, the sooner I can figure out if I managed to call Anna and warn her that I'd be out.

"You don't have to do this," Mom says. "You can go home and rest."

I ignore her and force my brain to retrieve the deputy's question, then the answer. "I thought there were monsters chasing me," I say. "It was a nightmare."

"So you ran into the woods?" the deputy asks.

"I had to get away from them." My head throbs, and each word takes a toll on me. "They were chasing me. I slipped while I was running and hit my head...... " It takes too much to put together sentences that don't sound ridiculous. Sharp pain shoots behind my eyes.

"Next thing I know, I'm in the cabin. I don't know how I got there."

Again, I fidget with the sleeves of my sweatshirt. I wish I could take it off, but it would only make them more suspicious of me.

"Was there anyone else in the cabin when you arrived?"

I close my eyes tight, then open them to get a clearer look at the deputy. She looks like the kind of person who manages to get a full night of sleep every night, who wakes up at seven a.m. and has a cup of coffee out of habit and not necessity. Must be nice.

"No. Just... " I breathe. "Just the mess."

The deputy responds, but it dissolves in the air before reaching me. The rhythm of blood in my ears drowns out her voice, pulls me out of my own body. I watch the room tilt, spilling my parents and the deputy into a void.

The Iceheart's words wrapped in Shelby's voice repeat over and over.

"My daughter did not have anything to do with the deaths. She's lucky to be alive," Mom interjects. Her voice breaks through the fog in my skull. "You should be looking for the real killer instead of traumatizing her even more. Hasn't she been through enough? Hasn't our family been through enough?" Her voice grows more and more uneven with every word.

"She's our only connection to these cases. I'm only following procedure. I assure you, I want to let her go home to rest as much as you do."

Mom and the deputy go back and forth for a little while longer, so I close my eyes and sink into the chair. Without the angry fluorescent light ripping my eyes apart, the pain in my head subsides a little.

I want to go home.

No, I need to go to work.

"Cara?"

I've missed something.

My head whips up as if attached to a string controlled by someone else.

"What?" I say.

"Have you taken any drugs?" the deputy asks.

"No."

He talks to my parents about nightmares and how they can manifest under severe stress, then suggests I see a therapist.

As if we can afford that.

"I would like to recommend you keep her home for a couple days," the deputy says to my parents.

"No," I say. "I have to work. I've already missed two days' pay. And I have school. I can't stay home."

"We'll talk about it when we get home," Dad says. I hope that means he won't take the deputy's advice. "Deputy, is that all for today?"

To be difficult, I don't give the deputy a chance to speak. "I'm done answering questions, so I'd like to leave." My mood darkens suddenly, and my blood boils at the thought of the deputy's accusations. She could ruin me. I want to pound my fists on the table, to scream my innocence until her ears bleed.

If word gets out that the police think I had something to do with the recent murders, that'll be it for me. People won't give me the benefit of the doubt. I'll be a pariah.

The new, unfamiliar aggression in me demands I correct the deputy's thinking, but Mom helps me up and guides me out of the room.

Outside, I release my balled fists. My palms ache from where my nails bit into the skin. My hands tremble. I don't get like that. I don't long for violence. Yet the anger crawled in, infected me, and left me ready to tear the deputy apart.

"I shouldn't have missed work," I say.

Dad starts the car. "I called the store. Anna said she'd get your shifts covered," he says.

Relief floods me for mere seconds, but the heat from the

car's vents chases it away. My senses fade again, and the fog in my head returns like steam on the mirror after a hot shower.

My parents talk amongst themselves as we drive home, while I sit in the backseat and comb through worries of the interrogation. I wish I could linger on not wanting to miss more school or work, but instead I hang onto the theories and accusations.

How could I have done that to those bodies? How does she think one girl could do something so gruesome?

I take my phone out of my pocket and look at my texts. Sometime yesterday I asked Mel if the kittens were okay, asked Lucas if he was okay, asked Anna if she had any shifts I could work to make up for lost hours.

Lucas and Mel responded quickly. They're fine. The kittens are fine.

An unread message from Anna sits at the top of the list.

I'm not going to mince words, Cara. I can't afford to have you representing my store while the rumors are floating around. You're a suspect in two murder investigations. People won't feel comfortable with you here. We will mail your last paycheck to your house. You're fired.

I read the paragraph again.

This has to be a mistake.

"Anna fired me," I say, not more than a whisper. "Because I'm a suspect in the murders. How does she know that? Does everyone know?"

"It's a small town. These things get around," Mom says.

"I didn't hurt them. I didn't hurt anyone, I swear."

Mom sighs over the crunching of tires on the sanded road. "I know you didn't. But people are scared, and they'll hold on to whatever answers they're given. You have to be strong. Imagine how many people thought your father and

I were failed parents when Shelby disappeared, but we didn't let them win."

I tighten my fists and curl my sore toes inside my boots. I don't deserve this. I don't know how to stop it. And how can my parents be fine with this? With people thinking their daughter might be a murderer? Why aren't they fighting this?

"Did the doctors find any drugs in my system?" I ask, weak. Afraid.

Dad taps his fingers on the steering wheel. "They don't know. They couldn't interpret the results."

I sit straighter in my seat. "What do you mean they couldn't interpret the results?"

"The test failed, Cara. They tried three different samples, and none of them made sense."

"What does that mean? They had to have found something."

Mom lets out a small sound in her throat.

"They did. Your blood contains microscopic ice crystals," he finally says, emotionless. "They found the same thing in your sister."

FORTY

I need you to lie for me, I text Lucas when my hands stop shaking long enough for me to type.

The message from Anna still lurks on my phone, and I've reread it a thousand times. I replay my entire time working for her, looking for ways I could've been better, ways I could have prevented this. My place in her favor could never have been permanent. I was still a teenager working for a woman who made up reasons to mistrust us, and, despite having done nothing wrong, she found a reason to mistrust me too.

What was once a solid plan for my future—especially since I'd been selected for the internship—has collapsed. I don't know what to do next.

Things have only gotten worse since Shelby came home. Her monster has been pulling at me, tearing me from school, from work, from every responsibility I painstakingly held onto for dear life. Her monster has done this to me. Whatever it is, whatever she brought here with her, it is the thing chipping away at my foundation.

What do you need? Lucas messages back.

Tell me this monster isn't going to kill me.

I sit on my bed, twirling my key ring on my middle finger and debating whether I should leave and get some air. A cup of coffee might help the aching in my head, and maybe if I ate something, I wouldn't feel so jittery.

Though, every time I think of eating, the image of a monster gnawing on bones makes me sick.

It won't. We'll figure this out.

The best thing about text messages is I can't hear the lie in Lucas's voice. Whatever sort of tell he has, I don't see it when he says what I want to hear. He can lie as much as he wants with the written word, and I can believe it all.

We should talk about what happened... he adds.

He's right. We should talk about it, but the thought of spilling all the details I remember terrifies me. What if he fills in the blanks of my memory with things I don't want to think about?

I suck in a long breath, but the air in the house sticks to my throat. Even with the heat as low as it can go before the pipes will freeze, I can't get comfortable.

I'm going for coffee. You could meet me there. I press send before I have a chance to change my mind. He can help me end this. He will help me get my life back to normal so I don't lose what little I have left of my plan.

I have nothing left to believe in except him.

ELEANOR'S BUSTLES with life from students recently freed from the confining walls of the school. They circle around tables with too few chairs for the number of people in their group, and resort to sitting on laps or squishing two bodies into one seat. Voices carry through the small space, collecting in a cloud in the center and blurring into noise.

There's an ice cream place in Riverside. It would have been quieter, but it has too many memories tied to it. Shelby and I would go there when we had something to celebrate—even small things, like getting a passing grade on an assignment or those teachers' work days we got off from classes. She always tried a new flavor, always the adventurer. I always got cookie dough.

I struggle to remember that Shelby now. How much of that girl remains inside the one that came back? Or was she telling the truth when she said there was nothing left?

At the counter, I grab a plastic-wrapped, day-old turkey sandwich from the cooler, and the guy working the register pulls a mug off the stack for my usual order of drip coffee—the cheapest caffeinated option.

"Wait," I say. "I want something different today."

He sets the mug back down.

"I'd like an iced latte." I prickle inside at the cost of the drink. Five dollars for espresso and milk. It feels frivolous, irresponsible. Especially now...

"Oh. Okay." His eyes fall to the thin sweater I wear. The skeptical expression on his face says he knows how the police found me in the woods.

"Extra ice," I say. I scan my card, then leave before he can hand me my receipt.

The guy keeps glancing back at me like I have a second head, and I glare back every time. I can't be the first person to order a cold drink in February, and I won't be the last. But this town is small, like Mom said, and there's no telling how the rumors skewed before they reached his ears.

"Hey," Lucas says when he appears beside me. "I got a table over there, when you're ready." He points to a table with two seats, one of which has a drink in a plain white mug set in front of it, and the other with his coat draped over the back.

"Okay. I'll be right there."

They guy from the counter gives me one last look as he hands me a glass with my latte.

"Iced?" Lucas asks. There is more to the question.

"Yep." I take a long drink to prove how much I enjoy the cold. It doesn't taste very good. "Iced." The temperature doesn't register on my tongue, only the sweetness of the drink.

I take a bite from my sandwich, neither satisfied nor dissatisfied by the slightly stale bread and cold meat inside. Lucas folds his hands around the cup in front of him and watches me, but doesn't speak. The food spreads energy through my body, and I realize I don't know how long it's been since the last time I ate. No wonder I feel so miserable.

"Are you doing okay?" he asks between sips of coffee.

"I don't... I don't know." I shake the ice in my cup, take another drink.

"Have you talked to Shelby at all?"

He speaks softly and meets my eyes with a look of worry. They scan my face for evidence of the things I hide from him. I do the same, searching the depths of his deep brown irises for a shred of information to latch onto.

"No. I can't. When I was out in the woods I... the monster. It showed me things. It put her voice in my head. I don't know." Too many things run circles in my head, too fast for me to linger on for longer than a second. "The doctors found ice in my blood. Apparently Shelby has it too."

"You can't withstand heat anymore, can you? That's why you're dressed like that."

I nod.

His mouth forms a line curved slightly downward, and he taps his fingers on the edge of his mug. "That makes sense."

Sweat coats the lines of my palms. "What does?"

"You kept seeing the Iceheart and it never attacked. It wasn't hunting you, it was testing you."

"For what."

He shakes his head. "It won't get to that point."

"Lucas," I demand.

He doesn't relent.

"If I had listened to you at the search party, when you first said you thought it was a monster, could I have saved her?" I ask.

"No."

A breath quivers in my throat, a death rattle, and I bring the latte to my lips. The glass slips from my shaking hands and shatters on the ground. Everyone in the room turns to me. They stare like the monsters did.

"Will this cold in me go away?"

"Do you want me to lie?"

"Only if the answer is no."

Lucas doesn't answer, and I know why. The cold in me will stay, dashing any hopes of moving somewhere warmer once I establish myself in the world. I can't move to Costa Rica like Shelby and I dreamed of doing before I lost her. The sun would burn me from the inside out like I'm some kind of vampire.

"My mom has the fever too. She's the only person I know who survived it," Lucas says. "Normally, the Iceheart shows you things. It likes to show off its kills. Victims eventually break from the nightmares and run out to meet their deaths in a fit of delirium. That's it. No questions whether you live or die. You just die."

"But she got away," I say.

"She killed it before it killed her."

"Is that what happened to your dad?" I ask.

"He thought he killed it, but didn't perform the ritual for proper disposal. He didn't banish the spirit, and it returned to the trees to find another host. It decided to take him."

I forget to breathe.

Sadness forms in the corner of Lucas's mouth. "He wanted a normal life for us. My mom had to... she hasn't been the same since. Defeating a monster that looked like that man she loved broke her."

"Will she tell you what to do with this one?"

"I have other resources for that. I don't need her to worry," he responds too quickly. He's been preparing the answer long before I asked the question. I let it go.

One of the employees comes to clean the spill, and Lucas and I sit in silence while they do.

"Listen. There was something else I needed to talk to you about," Lucas says when the employee leaves. "I need you to step back and let me work on this alone. It's too dangerous for you."

"You're just deciding this now? Why couldn't you have said that before? Maybe then I wouldn't have this fever."

"Just, let me handle this. The police are watching you now, and I don't need their attention. Keep a candle lit, and I'll tell you when it's done."

"But—"

"This isn't a negotiation. I'm the hunter. I know what I'm doing."

FORTY-ONE

The thought of being alone makes me uneasy, especially now. Mel's house sits so deep in the woods, it would be the perfect place for the monster to come for me. But I don't have a choice. Lucas has ignored me for the past two days. I thought he'd still talk to me, but my texts sit on my phone unanswered and he blatantly avoids me in the halls at school.

I swing the truck into Mel's driveway and check the woods before I cut the engine and park. Enough light remains for me to see between the trees, and I find nothing. Nothing I can see, at least.

Hope barks once inside, and it startles me so bad I jump. The sound breaks out against the deathly quiet forest and scatters birds from the trees into the sky.

When I go inside, the dog looks at me from the corner of her eyes like she doesn't recognize me. Mel looks from the dog to me, eyebrows furrowed tight and a frown across her mouth.

"You look awful," she says. "Are you sure you don't want to go home and rest?"

"No. No, I'm okay." I need the distraction, the illusion of normalcy. "I don't want to be at home."

The heat in the house sets fire to my bones, and I peel my jacket off. Sweat gathers on my neck where the leather collar once touched my skin, hot and uncomfortable, and I brush it away with the edge of my T-shirt.

"Just call me if you need to go home, okay?" Mel asks.

"Sure." I won't call. I won't need to go home.

She looks at me with disbelief, then takes the dog and disappears through the door.

I go to the kitten room and sit cross-legged on the floor. The kittens, even Paisley, don't recognize me right away. They hide the way they do when the Iceheart lurks outside. My eyes sting, and I pinch them shut. Something's different about me, and the cats can tell.

"It's just me," I say in the softest voice I have. It still breaks. "You know me."

I reach for them, hoping they will recognize the scent of me. Paisley still flinches when my hand gets close to her, and it sends a knife through my heart. I have never felt more alone than I do now. Everyone in town thinks I'm a murderer. Lucas thinks I'm a liability. The kittens think I'm a monster.

The four kittens watch me from a safe corner of the room, curious but not curious enough to come closer. Not after I tried to touch Paisley.

I take a textbook out of my backpack and open it to the first chapter I have to read. The words smudge on the page and I can't process their meaning, so I turn page after page to trick myself into thinking I'm being productive. I'm not.

My fingertips go numb and fumble with the pages I need to turn. I rub my hands together to warm them, but the friction burns my skin.

I dig my phone out of my backpack to search for the symptoms I feel, but it won't unlock. The touchscreen doesn't register the presence of my fingers on its surface, so I press harder as if the thing operates based on force and not sensing heat. Needless to say, it doesn't work.

"Okay, then." I toss the phone aside and look again at the kittens, who should be climbing all over me.

My thoughts consume me, and I lose myself in them. I wonder if the hunters know what to do about this fever, wonder how to find another of them who might help me.

Slowly, I drift to the place between sleep and dreams, where my subconscious grows stronger until it takes control. It digs up memories I wanted to forget, things I saw and ruled out as a fever dream.

The signs of death have been cleaned up from the cabin when it forces its way back into my mind. No more blood-stains on the floor with footprints through the dark puddles. Someone has swept away shreds of torn flannel and canvas, and it's as though everything I found here before had been an illusion. A trick.

I can't get out, can't get back to Mel's, to reality.

Could this be a form of reality?

I'm sorry you have to see this. I'm sorry. I'm sorry. I'm so sorry, fake-Shelby says in my head. The apology repeats, skipping.

The wind whistles off the side of the cabin, and the trees around me sing sorrowful songs to slow my blood until it moves through my veins like a glacier. I'm there again, standing by the Christmas-plaid couch and staring into the face of the moose head mounted on the wall.

I'm sorry. I'm sorry. I'm so sorry.

A door swings open behind me, and the wind dies down. The creature, far too big for the doorframe, ducks inside the cabin with a new victim. Its long, bony fingers hold one of the boy's ankles and drags it into the cabin. There are remnants of the forest in the boy's dark hair, dirt smeared on his cheek and neck.

"Don't make me watch this," I plead. But this is a dream, and no one can hear me.

The boy stirs. He isn't dead yet.

Wild animals surround him, licking their chops and waiting for permission to feed. They glance up at their master for a sign it doesn't give. The Iceheart fixates on the boy.

The boy wakes, rubbing his eyes and groaning from the ache he must have from being dragged through the brush.

His eyes widen at the sight of the pack in front of him, but he doesn't get a chance to scream.

"No." The monster can't hear me.

The animals do not listen.

"Please. Stop."

I cannot stop this.

I cannot wake.

The monster rises to its full height and lets out the last sound this boy will ever hear. The shriek punctures my eardrums and hot blood rolls down my jawline. Even the predators cower beneath the sound and back away from the monster's meal.

I can't move.

The monster takes one final step toward the boy, and I want to wake up so I won't have to see this.

"No," I plead.

The boy holds his hands up as he tries and fails to scramble away, but the thin limbs are nothing against the monster's claws. Bones snap beneath the impact, then the Iceheart goes for the soft flesh of his stomach. Blood and organs spill from the wound, staining his clothes a deep red.

The sound of the Iceheart feeding makes me sicker than the sight of the gore, and shivers tear through my body.

This is a nightmare. This is a nightmare.

The Iceheart looks up from the boy for a minute and its face is entirely red.

This is real, fake-Shelby says. *This is happening, and you can't stop it.*

Why is it using her voice? Isn't making me watch this bad enough? Why is it doing this to me?

The monster dives back into the boy's abdomen and tears at flesh. The animals squeal and yip with excitement for what unfolds before them. The ground shakes beneath me from their movement.

The boy goes limp not long after the Iceheart begins its feast.

When I blink, the cabin, the blood, the animals all fade and my brain reassembles the kitten room. The cats are nowhere to be found, which tells me all I need to know. My screams weren't only in the nightmare.

The room flickers in and out, and my whole body tingles with icy numbness when I try to stand—to prove to myself that I *can* stand—but there is nothing solid in my body. I black out before I hit the floor again.

FORTY-TWO

Mom made Shelby's favorite meal—an elaborate breakfast spread with waffles, sausage, scrambled eggs, raisin toast, and fruit—for Tuesday dinner, because my sister hadn't eaten in days. I offered to bring it to Shelby's room when she didn't appear at the table, but the fact that the smell of butter and syrup didn't draw her out of hiding said enough. She wasn't going to eat it.

I knocked on the door, but didn't wait for her to answer before I let myself in.

The cold air hit me hard, and I noticed the window by her bed open a few inches. She huddled up next to it, like someone dying of a fever who wanted nothing more than to taste the chill once more.

"Shut that," I demanded. "You're letting the heat out."

Shelby glared at me, and opened the window another half inch.

"I can't breathe with it closed," she said.

I sat at the edge of her bed and she squirmed away from me, curling up tighter by the window.

"You need to eat," I said, and gestured to the plate I set on her nightstand. "Mom made your favorite. She even got fresh berries instead of frozen."

Shelby turned up her nose at the plate.

My sister's skin had turned gray, and her eyes held no light in them. Near her mouth, thin lines had begun to carve their place around a frown.

"Do you want to talk about Parker?" I asked.

No answer.

"It's okay to be upset. You can still not want someone to die, even if you're angry with them."

The words resonated a little too much with how I felt about my sister. I wanted her to be okay, deep down, despite how badly I wanted to take her by the collar and shake some sense into her.

I swallowed the swollen, unwelcome feelings.

She looked out at the forest, facing the near-icy stream of cold like a dog with its head out the car window.

My own stomach growled with every question I asked, every reassuring bit of advice I offered. Eventually, I let my own hunger win and left her there in her room. It felt strange being the one to walk away—too new, too unlike me—but I couldn't stay anymore.

FORTY-THREE

Lucas's house looks different from the doorstep.

Up close, the sage green paint curls and flakes away from the side of the house, and a metal knocker decorated with an elaborate sword and the name *Powell* hangs in the center of the pumpkin-colored door. The knocker is the only thing on this house hinting at the lives of the family inside. Everything else matches the generic features of newer developments in town.

I don't know what made me decide to come here. I don't know what I'll do if Lucas is home.

I didn't come here to talk to him.

The sound of the knocker meeting its base echoes through the silent morning, and sends a shiver down my spine as if it could alert the Iceheart of my presence. Would it come for me in the brightness of midmorning?

The door creeps open, revealing the tired face of Lucas's mother. I remember her from that day at the police station, tan skin with a grayish pallor, dark hair with streaks of frazzled white. "Hello?"

"Hi, Mrs. Powell. I'm sorry to bother you, but I... I need to talk to you."

She looks at me, perplexed at why I'm here and not at school like I should be. "You're the girl whose sister disappeared."

It's been a while since someone called me that, but it still fits. "She came back."

"Oh. That's wonderful. They don't usually come back, do they?"

I shake my head.

"How is she recovering?"

Lucas's mother has no idea what's happened with my sister. How could he have kept that from her?

"She isn't. She's really sick." I have to shift the conversation before I lose my nerve. "Is there somewhere we could sit?"

She tells me I can call her Jasmine, then takes me into the kitchen and offers me one of three chairs at the circular dining room table. The fourth has been tucked against the wall where the table has been folded in to make more space in the room. A round, orange cat sits on the place setting for that spot, and it looks at me with yellow eyes.

"Watch that one. He's a thief." She points to the cat. "You're eyeing that keychain, aren't you, Murray?"

My hand goes instinctively to my keys. He can't have them.

"There's another one around here somewhere. I hope you don't mind cats."

"Um. Cats mind me, lately," I say, but she doesn't notice. "But listen, I need your help."

Her expression darkens, eyes like pools of ink set deep in her skull, and in that moment I see Lucas in her. She knows I know something I shouldn't based on the way her posture goes tense as she lowers herself into the seat across from me.

"How do you think I can help?" she asks, obviously well-practiced in extracting information without giving too much away.

"Lucas told me about your family," I begin.

Her expression doesn't change, no shock or surprise or anger that her son would expose their secret.

"He's been helping me. Or, well, he was... but he's been ignoring me since"—I breathe—"since the monster we were looking for took me into the woods."

She brings a hand over her mouth, long fingers covering the lower half of her face so I can't see her reaction.

I tell her everything, trying to string together shreds of information in a way that makes sense, but it isn't easy. Lucas left so many gaps in my knowledge, and I don't understand some of the things he told me well enough to explain to another person.

Her face finally changes, eyes wide in understanding.

"He wasn't supposed to be hunting alone," she finally says after dragging seconds of silence. "He isn't finished with his training. He wasn't even training for extermination, not after what happened to his father."

"What do you mean?"

"We begin our training at ten, and choose a focus at thirteen. He chose the scholar path, because that was less dangerous than extermination or field work."

My stomach drops and my heart follows. "He said he could help me. He said he knew what to do. I didn't know what else to do."

Jasmine waves a hand. "He should have brought you to me. My son knows the protocols for this kind of thing. Don't blame yourself for trusting him."

She radiates such cold, sharp disappointment that even the cat notices and hops down from the table where it won't freeze.

I fiddle with something on the table, the cap from a bottle of pop, and avoid Jasmine's eyes. I don't want her to have to reassure me this isn't my fault, but I accept the words. I cling to them. This isn't my fault.

"Has he told you what he thinks it is?"

The blood drains from my face, and I struggle to maintain eye contact.

"Lucas thought it had a connection to me, because it's been following me." I give her all the details I have: how it follows me, how it lured me into the woods, how it made me sick. She listens wordlessly as I regurgitate the last three weeks onto her table but still manage to avoid its name.

She doesn't need me to say it. With every word, I drive the stake in deeper. The sickness, the cold, the visions. Everything. She knows this is the thing that tore her family apart.

"Thank you for coming to me," Jasmine finally says. She holds herself together, but a twitch in her tightened jaw says she won't be able to hide whatever she really feels for long. "I'll get someone out here to handle this. In the meantime, I need you to stay away from it if you can."

Jasmine won't say its name either.

"And if it shows up, you call or text me."

"But I can't. My hands... the phone doesn't work," I say.

She digs through a drawer and retrieves a small, thin object. A stylus. The kind that mimics heat on a touchscreen. Then she hands me a card with her number on it. No details, only a phone number.

"Listen to me, Cara. Those nightmares you've been having aren't nightmares. The Iceheart shows you its kills as they unfold. It wants to break your mind so it can take over. It's grooming you to be its next host, which means it's weak. Its old host is dying, and that makes it easier for us to kill."

It's grooming me to be its next host. I hold on to that for a few minutes before I try and process it. Turns out, I can't. Can't ask Jasmine if she experienced the same thing. Can't ask her how she got through this. Can't ask her if the monster might lead me into the woods again. Can't even settle on a question worth asking, because I don't want to know the answer. I don't want this.

FORTY-FOUR

ack at school, pandemonium fills the hallways around me. I stand to the side by my locker, taking in conversations I wasn't invited to. A girl with purple and blue braided into her bleached hair heaves words past her lips like weights, and her friends try to calm her with inaudible reassurance.

Someone else has died, but I knew that already.

The way the atmosphere clings to me, stale and burdensome, tells me enough. Emotions floating through the air buzz in my ears like static.

But the worst part is waiting for the details I fear will come, the ones that make me feel guilty for the horrible things I didn't do, but didn't stop either. I already know every excruciating detail.

The Iceheart showed me, and I did nothing.

A wave of anger surges through me, and sweat collects in all the places the fabric of my clothes meets skin. Voices around me blur except for the girl with purple hair. Hers stands out, because I can't help hoping she might say something else that won't feel so damning.

"They found his license near a body in the cabin where they found those hunters," the girl says. "What was he doing out there?"

Her voice rises and falls, uneven, a girl on the verge of a breakdown. The deceased meant something to her, but I don't remember what she said barely a minute prior. Was it her brother? A cousin? A boyfriend, maybe? The boy the Iceheart showed me last night would be the right age for any of those things.

Oh god, I could have stopped this.

Lucas could have stopped this too, and he didn't. He could have called for help and this could have been over by now. How many of the dead would still be here if he'd done that right away?

The girl's friend looks away from her and fixes her gaze on me. She scowls at me, then guides the group away from where I stand.

Over the intercom, someone at the front office calls for me. Everyone in the hall freezes, searching for me in the crowd.

"Maybe she's finally getting arrested," someone says.

"I wonder how she did it. She doesn't look all that strong," says another.

I grind my teeth as I walk, head down, past my classmates, and try ignoring the things they say.

"She was at all the crime scenes, and her sister used to party at that cabin before Parker died."

"Maybe she killed Parker."

"Maybe she tried to kill her sister."

The accusations should be lethal, but I'm still upright by the time I reach the office, where two sheriff's deputies wait for me. One, a ruddy-faced man I vaguely recognize, stands with his thumbs hooked in his belt, and the other,

Deputy Mendes, has her arms crossed. Neither of them looks impressed to have to be here.

The principal guides the deputies and me into one of the administrative rooms, then tells me Dad is on his way. Great. Just great.

"Can you tell us where you were last night?" Deputy Mendes asks. Her eyes bore into me, searching for a weak point to take advantage of.

"I was at my friend Mel's house, watching her foster kittens."

Mendes writes that down, along with Mel's last name and phone number when I offer it. I have an alibi. I wasn't out killing people.

But maybe Mel won't want me in her home after the police contact her. Maybe she'll cut me out of her life too. Then I'd really have nothing to lose.

"And where were you this morning before you got to school?" the deputy asks.

"I wasn't feeling well, so I slept in a bit." It doesn't seem right to send the police to Jasmine, so I lie.

"Are you aware there was another incident at the cabin where you were found last week?" the other deputy asks.

"I heard. People have been talking about it."

"If you have any information to share, it's in your best interest to do so."

"I was at Mel's house, then went straight home. I don't have anything else to tell you." My voice sounds almost confident despite how shaky I feel on the inside.

Dad comes in just as the deputies close their notepads, accepting that I won't talk to them anymore. They acknowledge him, but don't ask further questions. Not in front of me, at least. For all I know, they may already have questioned him.

"Everything okay?" Dad asks when the police are gone.

"Obviously not. But I didn't do what they think I did."

He leans forward in the seat beside mine, elbows on his knees in that stereotypical Dad way. On a normal day, he'd be asleep right now, and he looks like he needs the rest desperately with one daughter under investigation for a string of murders and the other completely off the rails.

"I know you didn't," he says.

"This is ruining my life." And just like that, I break for the first time since Shelby disappeared. "I can't do this anymore."

He tries to console me, reassuring me that the people who matter don't think I did anything wrong, and the people who do think that aren't important. The warmth of his tentative hug smothers me, and I try to break free though I want the comfort so bad. Is this how Shelby felt when she came home? Did she want the comfort of her family but couldn't survive the warmth?

I stop crying abruptly when a realization hits me. All the things Jasmine said about the Iceheart grooming me to be its next host, the ice in mine and my sister's blood, the hours Shelby spent unaccounted for in the middle of so many nights.

"Oh no," I say before I can stop myself.

Oh no, no, no. Please, god, let me be wrong.

FORTY-FIVE

The light by the front door has died.

I walk inside guided by the bright screen of my phone and the glow of a distant lamp. The eerie, uneven illumination makes the house feel more sinister now, positioning shadows that could be monsters all around me.

This place used to be home, but the thing disguised as Shelby has ruined it. It twisted my life until it became unrecognizable. If it hadn't come, I wouldn't have lost my job, wouldn't have lost the internship, and wouldn't be a suspect in a serial murder case. I wouldn't have spent the last four hours at Mel's house trying to convince the kittens I am the same person I was before this all went to hell. Of course, they didn't listen. They know better. I'm not the same, and I can't go back.

I toyed with texting Jasmine and telling her my theory, but I couldn't. I have to see this for myself first. It gives me more time to be wrong. Please let me be wrong about this. Please.

Shelby waits in the kitchen, pacing back and forth across the linoleum and muttering nonsense to herself. When she notices me, she greets me and asks about my day. She hasn't been friendly since returning home, and this feels wrong. It feels too practiced and sweet like she's luring me in.

"Another kid was murdered," I say, matter of fact. "By your monster."

By you, my mind repeats.

She rearranges her expression into a frown, but it doesn't even look like her. She never used to frown so deeply. She'd press her mouth into a thin line, lips tucked in like hiding them meant she wasn't upset.

This thing has my sister so wrong. I should've noticed sooner.

"That's awful," she says.

I glare at her, annoyed she can't read my mind. She should know I think she's full of shit.

I pull a pop from the fridge and leave her there, hoping she will follow me into my room to continue the conversation she thinks we're having.

She does, and I set my pop on the nightstand behind the candle I've kept lit every night despite how miserable it makes me feel. I pick up the lighter and hide it in the sleeve of my sweater. The Iceheart isn't the only one with tricks.

"What do you want?" I ask as I turn.

"I want you to trust me. You're my sister."

The words hurt, because, if I'm right, my sister is dead. I have no closure, nothing to finalize her death. But she'll still be gone. Still dead.

"Prove it, then. Prove that I can trust you," I say.

"How?"

"Close your eyes."

She does as I ask, though her face looks strained in the seconds before they close. A vein in her forehead bulges slightly, like the simple task of shutting her eyes takes more effort than it should.

Please let me be wrong about this.

I take her hand in mine and lift it into the space between us. Her skin is as cold as my own, cold like the dead.

With her eyes closed and the vein relaxed, my sister looks at peace. Like a body laid out in a casket for one final look before being placed in the ground. Her ghostly white skin, dry and flaky, relaxes, and her scarred mouth curves slightly upward, as if for this moment she is content.

I flick the lighter and bring life to the flame, then hold it close to her hand. She flinches, uncomfortable by the slight heat of the little fire. Deep lines spread across her face as she resists the thing that lives inside her.

With my grip tight on her hand, I move the flame closer to her.

She pinches her eyes tighter. Her upper lip exposes her teeth as she winces from discomfort, and her teeth look sharper, and longer when she shows them.

"What are you doing?" she asks.

I hold her hand tighter to keep her from slipping out of my sweaty grasp.

"Finally getting answers from you," I say.

Beads of sweat break out on her forehead and slide down her cheeks and neck. She thrashes her hand out of my grip, suddenly stronger.

This probably wasn't the best idea, but I stick with it through the flame burning my thumb.

I keep tormenting the thing that's been tormenting me

for weeks. It took my sister, my home, and my ability to feel close to anyone. It deserves this.

"Stop."

Her eyes open, revealing not the borrowed brown ones belonging to Shelby, but the sickening red ones of the Iceheart. They peel back her eyelids and carve themselves free from the confines of her skull, and smear down her face.

"*Stop.*"

She knocks the lighter from my grip with a partially shifted hand. Her nails have disappeared, and the skin of her fingertips strains gray from the pressure of bones trying to break free. Her knuckles pop and stretch as she closes her fingers around my wrist.

I freeze, terrified of what comes next. Will this thing shift and kill me in my home?

I expect it to speak, but instead, it locks its gaze on mine, blinding me, and says nothing. No threats. No lies. Shelby's lips curl open in a hungry grin, and the teeth I thought looked sharper have transformed into daggers.

I can't move.

I stare down at the malformed hand around my wrist and will it to loosen its grip.

"Let me go." I mean to be strong, but my voice comes out fragile, terrified.

Instead of killing me, the monster, drenched in sweat, rushes from my room and down the hall. The kitchen door slams shut as it runs, shrieking, into the trees.

I fall to the floor, knees bending at odd angles as I slump against the side of my bed. Charlie's tail twitches and brushes my fingertips from where she hides beside an old shoe box full of junk. Her presence tells me this was real. My suspicion was right. I can't deny it.

I watched my sister—no, I watched the *monster*—shed its skin and become the thing from my nightmares, the thing from the forest.

Another shriek comes from the woods outside my house, sending tremors through my bones.

FORTY-SIX

The truck was gone when I came out to the kitchen for coffee. Mom had already left for work and Dad was dead asleep after having gotten home a little over an hour before.

Shelby hadn't left a note this time, though I looked.

As bad as I felt, I wandered into the living room where Dad slept on his stomach to ask if he could drive me to school. Of course Shelby didn't think of how whatever she was doing would impact anyone else. Of. Fucking. Course.

Dad groaned as I interrupted his sleep.

"I'm really sorry to wake you up," I said.

"Oh, I was just resting my eyes." Typical Dad. "What's up?"

"Shelby left and I don't have a ride to school."

He didn't ask where she went, but the lines in his forehead deepened as he frowned before answering. "My keys are in my coat pocket. Keep it under the speed limit."

When I left a half hour later, Dad hadn't gone back to

sleep. He sat on the edge of his bed with his phone to his ear and one pajama-clad leg bouncing up and down.

I don't think he heard me say goodbye when I left the house the same way I always did lately. Alone. Dressed in layers and my leather jacket. Coffee in one hand and my backpack slung over the opposite shoulder. Funny how quickly a change in routine could turn into a new normal.

When I got to school, I drove around the parking lot a couple of times in search of Shelby's truck. Every black tail-gate sparked relief in my chest, only to be missing the dent Shelby put in it when she accidentally backed into a tree. Every Dodge grille belonged to a noticeably nicer vehicle, too new or too shiny or just not speckled with black spots from a half-assed paint job. Every truck that wasn't hers made my heart sink a little deeper in my chest.

I didn't know why I thought she'd go back to school, after everything, so I pulled Dad's car into the first open spot and leaned my forehead on the steering wheel.

Worry made itself home in my stomach and ate away at any strength I had left. I already knew what Shelby had done. It was inevitable, but it still sucked.

Maybe I should have called Dad or Mom or the police and told them so she didn't have as much of a head start, so we could catch up to her and bring her home, but I didn't. She'd have only left again if we caught up to her then.

I sat in the parking lot with Dad's Honda still running and counted the seconds it took to dull the ache in my chest telling me my sister had left. She was gone like she always wanted.

FORTY-SEVEN

I don't remember how to breathe on my own, so I count slowly to steady myself. But the breaths come in jagged, desperate bursts even still, and I keep losing track. I get to three, sometimes four, before I see Shelby transform again. Her eyes go from brown to red in an instant. Her teeth sharpen and her bones extend. She goes from my sister to a monster before my eyes. Over and over and over.

It keeps me from sleeping, and from functioning. I sit awake with fists clenched around the blankets on my bed and process the image on repeat.

Charlie sits on my desk across the room and looks at me, confused and untrusting. Her green eyes take me in, and her tail flicks with curiosity. She doesn't know I'm me. I wonder if she can tell the difference between the monster in me and the monster in Shelby—if there even is any difference.

I direct my mind somewhere else. Jasmine has cats, and they didn't seem anywhere near as put off by me. Maybe the kittens and Charlie need time, that's all, and they'll recognize me again.

The screen of my phone doesn't register my thumbprint, and I remember I have to use the stylus. This will take some getting used to. I unlock the phone and open a text to Jasmine.

I need to tell her what I know. It will help.

I ask about her cats instead, if their behavior changed when the Iceheart infected her too.

The message takes a while to send, and I realize it's three a.m. Time passes all wrong these days. It either passes too fast to process, or not at all, and I feel like I'm running out. How much longer do I have? How much longer does Shelby have?

My sister is the host. I type.

Delete it.

Type it again.

My sister is the host.

Delete.

Breathe.

Type it a third time.

My sister is the host.

Send.

Then I wait, and it feels like the rest of my life.

INSTEAD OF GOING TO SCHOOL, I go see Jasmine again. My discovery has changed things. I can't wait and hope the Iceheart doesn't come for me, because it lives in my house. It knows what I know.

"You know how vampires die by a silver bullet, fairies

by iron, yes?" is the first thing Jasmine says when I sit at the far end of her couch, and I'm too tired to be further exhausted by how very Lucas the question is.

"I guess." I thought wooden stakes killed vampires. I didn't think anyone would have a reason to kill a fairy.

"They are pure metals. Pure metals have healing properties dating back centuries for things as common as menstrual cramps. Our scholars have taken generations of experience and determined that some creatures are defeated through force, others through ritual, and others through the use of a specific weapon."

"Okay…"

"The Iceheart is the latter."

From behind her back, she draws a knife in a black leather pouch and hands it to me. I don't want to look at it, don't want to acknowledge the weight of the metal in my hands.

"If it comes for you, the heart is its weak spot. It has to be this dagger or one of its sisters, or the monster will simply heal around whatever weapon you use."

"But… I can't stab my sister. My parents, they'll know. They won't understand. I have to tell them why."

"It's not your sister. Not anymore."

"It looks like her. My parents think it's her. This will kill them."

"You can't share what you know. Not yet. The hunters I called are on their way. They'll have the situation handled within the week, and then we'll come up with a cover story."

A surge of energy rushes through me. "No. My family already lost Shelby once. You can't expect me to let you lie to them."

Jasmine's face goes serious, eyes sharp with something I don't recognize. "Do you want to know how I got this fever? Don't you wonder how I could have faltered up against this monster I was trained to destroy?"

I hadn't thought about it. I've only been thinking of myself, my sister, my family.

"If a woman of hunter blood marries, her husband swears an oath to follow in her footsteps. He takes her name. He declares loyalty to something he can never understand quite the same as those of us born into it. Lucas's father loved me more than he hated the idea of the work I did, so he joined us. He trained for years to become a hunter too, because to him there was romance in us taking down beasts as a pair. We came up against an Iceheart, but we didn't know what it was then. It took him like it took your sister, used his face to keep me unaware of how close it was, and it tried to take me too when his body wore out."

She doesn't look at me and instead keeps her gaze on the polished weapon I hold in my hands. Her words are measured, each pause calculated so she won't lose her cool. I know the way she speaks because I've done it myself. I've carefully planned responses to even the simplest questions to hide how badly Shelby's disappearance ruined me.

"It looked like him when it began to shift, and, even as a monster, I still knew exactly whose heart my knife would pierce. But he was dead the moment it settled into his bones, and your sister was dead the moment it settled into hers. Don't you think your parents will be better not knowing exactly what she became? Wouldn't you erase the sight of her changing, if you could?"

I don't need to say anything. Of course I would erase it. I never wanted to know any of this.

"Don't make me watch. I've seen enough blood already," I say.

Jasmine nods, agreeing to my terms. Her hunters will deal with this. All I need to do is stay alive.

FORTY-EIGHT

My body may be in the classroom, but my mind wanders. I think of morbid things, of death and loss and the holes they leave behind once the shock wears away. I think of monsters and how they used to be no more than stories to me, tales parents tell their kids about creatures who will get them if they misbehave. Monsters were only campfire hyperbole, bad things in legends to remind people to not be careless in the woods.

They weren't real.

But now I have to accept the truth. My sister left one day, and I thought the wound had finally healed. Instead, it became a scar that ached every time something reminded me of its existence until I eventually got used to the pain left in her wake. It didn't matter that sometimes memories blurred my vision and left me shaking, because I had no choice but to keep on living.

I learned to survive with a huge piece of me stolen away. Getting used to it—getting used to what became hot anger—was better than forgetting.

When nobody gave me proof of her death, I decided she

was alive somewhere she meant to go. Lost to us, but not to herself. I know now that she'd been alone, far north into the coldest corner of the world. Her secrets died with her. The Iceheart consumed them when it took her.

"Miss Hughes," the teacher says from the front of the room, "what were your thoughts on the themes of the story?"

I blink at her, forgetting what class I'm in, and what story I was supposed to read.

"I didn't read it," I say.

Humiliation doesn't bother me anymore. Whatever reading the teacher assigned doesn't matter anymore. She can fail me if she wants. Maybe I'll even be alive to feel the sting of it.

I tune back out before she responds because I don't care what lesson she's trying to teach.

A creeping cold like frigid lake water moves up my left hand, despite the oppressive heat of other students' bodies. The arm doesn't respond when I try to shake the feeling back into it. It sits on my desk, heavy as stone. I shake it with my right hand until it wakes, but the fingers at the end of it feel like they belong to someone else, the veins feel like they're filled with glue.

"You went to my mother."

Lucas appears behind me at my locker, and shutting the metal door on my head seems like a good alternative to turning around and talking to him. The first words out of his mouth make it seem like I betrayed him, as if he wasn't the one who left me to deal with this on my own.

I shake my left hand—cold slithering in again—then

turn with the kind of confidence born from having nothing left to lose.

"Well, the guy I was working with bailed on me so…… "

"You should know better. She's sick. She can't do this work anymore."

"I don't know that she'd appreciate you treating her like she's incapable of doing her job. She's the hunter, after all, and she's been very helpful. You're barely a scholar."

His face flushes like he didn't expect me to know that.

"She told me a lot of interesting stuff, really. I knew you were an asshole, but I didn't realize you were a liar and a fraud." The words pour from my mouth without any sort of provocation and I could set fire to this boy. "She had to kill a monster that looked like the man she loved, and how do you honor that? Oh, right. Put yourself in a position to get hurt too. That's great. I'm sure she'd rather keep your stupid territory than keep her stupider son."

"Cara, please. Stop." Lucas's eyes dart from side to side, looking for people who might have heard too much.

I don't care who hears. Let them think he's a dick.

"Were you going to tell me?" I ask.

The palm of my right hand itches and I clench it into a fist. God, I would love to hit him. He deserved it the first time and he'd deserve it even more today.

"No," he says. "I wasn't."

"What about Shelby? Did you know? Did you know what she is?"

His gaze hardens, eyes like a starless night, and he sets his jaw. He didn't expect me to fight back. Lucas expected me to back down like he told me to, and maybe the old me would have, but now I have nothing left to save but myself.

"Do you know what my sister has become?" I ask again, harsher and colder.

"A monster," he says.

I grab the collar of his shirt in my fist and push him into a row of lockers. It catches him off guard, and he stumbles, loses his balance, and slides to the floor.

"She's dead, Lucas. You let me believe she was alive, but she's been dead this entire time."

My grip tightens on his shirt and oh god, it would feel so good to hit him, but people have started to gather around us. Unwelcome voices reach my ears, hazy and toxic, and they say all the things I expect from the people in this school.

"She's probably going to kill him, too."

"Just make out already!"

"Get your camera out. Seriously."

"What if she kills him right here?"

"Looks like he likes it rough."

I release the fabric and Lucas scrambles to his feet. Before he gets a chance to leave, I push through the crowd. They part around me, afraid I might kill them too, so I take advantage of their fear to avoid the sticky, sick heat that lingers on me when I bump them.

When I get to the truck, I hold my breath and tear out of the parking lot with squealing tires. I drive too fast, but still can't put enough distance between me and the school. The crowd's comments fade until they become white noise around Lucas saying Shelby's a monster. His expression is burned in my head, dark eyes and tight jaw.

He knew.

He knew all along, and he didn't tell me.

I pull over somewhere between school and Mel's and slam my fists on the steering wheel, screaming my lungs raw until I have nothing left in me.

FORTY-NINE

I sit in Mel's driveway and wonder how long Lucas had been waiting for a monster to come and ravage this town so he could be the hero, and how long could he have kept it from the other hunters before someone realized the danger? How did Jasmine and the others not know, after all the deaths in the woods?

How could this have gotten so out of control?

"Why'd you stop bringing your friend?" Mel asks when I walk through the door.

"Project's done," I say. It isn't really a lie—we had been working on something together, just not the kind of project Mel thinks.

"You don't like him much, do you?" she asks.

"We're not friends," I say, still shaky from earlier. "We were stuck together."

She groans. "I used to hate it when that happened. The worst!"

"Tell me about it."

The conversation should feel normal, but a nagging

thought in the back of my mind says that even though Mel hasn't abandoned me yet, there's still time.

I hide away in the kitten room out of habit, though they still don't trust me. If I were to take a break, now would be the time, but I keep coming because if I stop I might never start again. This is all I have left of my old life.

My arm goes numb again, worse than it was at school. Always worse. Shaking it to regain feeling stops working eventually, or maybe it never did.

Jasmine's dagger sits sheathed at my waist. I wanted to keep it on me all day, but didn't wear it to school. Obviously. People think I'm a serial killer, so I don't need them discovering the blade—long as my forearm.

I take it from the sheath and drag it along my palm like people do in movies. All the nerve endings concentrated in the small space should tickle at the light touch, and they should scream when I press the blade down hard enough to break the skin.

The wound doesn't even bleed. It doesn't heal itself, but not even a thin line of blood collects in the cut. I try another, higher up the arm. Nothing. Just layers of pale skin sliced open like raw meat, like an autopsy. The limb has died.

THE ROOM MELTS away and another vision takes a hold of me. I've been waiting for the Iceheart to take me away again.

This time, it doesn't bring me to the cabin. It stands out against a pure blanket of snow. From the line of snow-dusted trees, a figure emerges, feet dragging, no jacket. Only a long gun, held pointed at the ground.

He doesn't get a chance to point the weapon at the creature luring him into its clutches. The boy collapses to his knees in the snow, and the weapon falls into the thick layer of powder beside him.

My blood goes still. I recognize this boy. As pissed off as I am and as much as he'd deserve it, I don't want Lucas to die.

Lucas doesn't have the right weapon to fight the Iceheart, even if he had the strength. My hand tightens around the handle of the dagger as if I can do anything from here.

"No," I breathe.

The vision cuts out, but the Iceheart is still in my head.

It's coming.

Time passes—minutes or days—and I dig through Mel's closet for her hunting rifle and a fistful of shells. My mind goes straight into panic mode as I load the gun as she showed me, but with only one useful hand, some of the ammunition falls to the floor between my knees.

The bullets aren't silver, but they'll have to do.

Back in the kitten room, I watch for the kittens to scramble to their hiding places. The Iceheart has to be coming for me. The presence of its fractured mind tingles through me.

When the kittens disappear, my blood goes still.

I have no choice but to go up against this thing now, alone, otherwise, it will do to me what it did to my sister. I'd rather die than let it make me a monster too, so I hold the rifle like someone who knows what they're doing, like someone who believes they stand a chance against the thing that's come to hunt them.

The lightness of the air outside almost brings me relief, but it's bittersweet. On one hand, I no longer have the weight of the warmth clinging to my lungs like anchors, but, on the other, my comfort in the cold was born of the thing I've come here to face.

I'm not ready.

I should have stayed inside.

I have the dagger, but I point the gun in the direction of the woods. Maybe I can do some damage. Slow it down. Something.

At least I'll keep it away from the kittens.

Red eyes appear between the trees, and no amount of preparation would stop the hairs on my arms and the back of my neck from rising. The Iceheart emerges first as a shadow, then a fully formed being.

I can't move.

Somewhere in my mind, I remember the gun and what I need to do.

I don't notice the car in the driveway behind me until lights cast the creature in a harsh brightness. It flinches, almost smeared out of existence with its shadows, but keeps coming at me on emaciated legs covered in rot. Already repulsive, the thing becomes so much worse under the blinding lights that expose details I hadn't processed before.

It looks nothing like my sister, like it never could have been her.

The skin covering its knees is stretched so thin, I expect it to burst. In some places, it already has—skin hanging limp like old paint on the side of a neglected home. Beneath the dangling flesh, I can make out hints of gray bone.

I glance behind me. Mel's Subaru sits in the driveway, idling. Her high beams leave me unable to see through her windshield.

"Hope. No! Come back here!"

Mel's voice breaks the silence.

The dog shatters the stillness.

Fuck.

The dog barrels past my legs, barking with all the force in her body. The monster turns its attention to her as she rushes closer, and the scarred skin grown over the Iceheart's mouth splits open with a scream.

FIFTY

Hope cowers beneath the sound of the Iceheart's shriek, but it doesn't deter her from rushing toward it. The thing is a threat. She needs to protect her person. She doesn't realize she can't win.

"Hope, get back here," Mel screams.

The dog doesn't listen and stops mere feet from the monster. She barks, a throaty sound from the bottom of her stomach, but the thing doesn't make a move for her.

I position the rifle on my dead hand, trying to mimic what Mel showed me so long ago, and use the other to curl a finger around the trigger.

"Hope, get back here. Now!" Mel's voice is frantic.

She takes a step toward the dog to pull it out of harm's way.

"Don't," I snap. "Don't go near it."

Hope continues snarling at the monster, which lowers itself on stretched limbs until it reaches the dog's level.

The gun kicks back into my shoulder when I pull the trigger the first time, and I see stars from the impact.

When my vision clears, I see the monster staggering back.

I pull the trigger again, sending a bullet straight into the center of its chest and opening a bloody wound. It exposes the monster's ribs, along with a heart encased in ice—a single canyon of a crack running across the shell.

A third bullet to the abdomen spills intestines, gray and wrinkled, onto the ground.

Strained skin around the opening relaxes away from where the bullets pierced. Liquid too clear to be blood oozes from its body with the other things the shots shook loose.

I have two bullets left.

Mel takes a chance and grabs the dog by the collar, dragging her away from the momentarily stunned monster.

"Go inside," I say.

"What the fuck is that?" Mel asks again.

"Go inside. It doesn't matter."

I pump another bullet into the monster, but I miss its chest. My aim fails without the use of my left arm.

One more bullet.

Then I'm defenseless.

The putrid scent of decay swirls through the air and into my nostrils. The rot smells worse today, like opening the thing's body let more of the stench out into the world. I taste it. Bitter and repulsive, the taste of medicine and spoiled food mixed together.

I shoot one last time, and the shot lands in the center of its chest and blows away bits of ribcage.

The Iceheart comes toward me again, and I pull the trigger though the weapon is empty. The bullets in my pocket won't do me any good because I can't load them.

So I drop the gun and take the dagger from its sheath.

The smell comes closer.

I hold my breath, awaiting pain.

The crack on the creature's heart undoes itself, smoothing over into flawless ice again. Even if I could reach the crucial organ, I couldn't get the dagger through the thick armor around it. Not now that it's healing before my eyes.

I only pissed it off.

A gunshot rings out in the distance, and I panic, thinking Mel has come back out. But I have her gun.

Another shot comes.

Three more.

The monster stops coming at me and collapses to one knee in the snow. It could've been my chance to kill it, had it been down for more than a moment.

From the forest, a figure emerges. Limping.

The Iceheart turns to Lucas like he shouldn't be upright, and moves toward the trees that spat him out into this fight.

It doesn't want him. I feel its annoyance mixed with my own emotions. Lucas is a distraction, an obstacle. It wants me. It needs me.

It's failing.

I don't know how Lucas got here. Don't know what happened between the vision I had earlier and now, but the lights from Mel's still-idling Subaru reveal a smear of blood trailing down his face from a wound at his temple. He carries a gun.

Lucas drags a leg as he comes closer to the monster, ignoring the blood streaming down his face and neck down the sweatshirt he wears.

I fish out a couple of shells from my pocket and shove two into the rifle, then hold it up to aim.

The Iceheart's mouth gapes open, blood and skin

clinging to where its scream tore free. Thick red liquid oozes down its chin, and an impossibly long tongue swipes the droplets away.

My bullet flies past the Iceheart.

It shoots a frigid glance at me, then turns its attention to Lucas.

The Iceheart's presence in my head pushes everything else out. It needs me. It needs a new host, a new body, but it is desperate now.

Lucas fires, then I do.

The monster screams again, louder and sharper than before, and a trail of hot blood trickles from my ears and eyes.

It can't take me tonight. Not with so many holes in its skin to heal.

Lucas falls into the snow, landing on his side. The Iceheart grabs him by a leg and drags him through the deep snow without another look back at me.

I collapse beside my rifle and watch the figure's silhouette fade away among the shadows.

The woods swallow the monster and Lucas in a single gulp. The trees take and take until nothing remains. My sister's life ended within them. So did the lives of four others. The trees will take Lucas next. He doesn't deserve this.

The monster lures and drags people into the dark places where the trails end and nobody goes, the trees watch in silence. They keep the secrets of the things living among them. They do not taste the things they consume, but they are always hungry for more. They will never be satisfied.

FIFTY-ONE

"Cara, get inside. You're going to freeze to death."

Mel drags me up by the elbow I can't feel and leads me inside. She doesn't know I can't freeze out here, or that the heat in her house feels like it might be the thing to kill me.

My body feels sluggish, heavy but at the same time hollow. The Iceheart's mind is gone from my head, though I search for the connection. I could find Lucas, probably, if I could just move.

"Do you know what that thing was?" she asks.

Her voice sounds far away, foggy. It sounds like she's asking the question of someone else, not me.

She scratches Hope's ears when we get inside, focusing on the shaking dog instead of me. The dog looks up at Mel, licking the drying tears from her cheek. Mel doesn't push the dog away and instead pulls Hope in closer.

"It's called the Iceheart." A language I don't speak passes my lips. "It's here because of Shelby."

I don't tell her it *is* Shelby.

"Why do you know its name?" Mel gets up from the

ground to get Hope some fresh water. While she's up, she takes a can of beer from the fridge with trembling hands and cracks the top. "Why aren't you more freaked out by this?"

Her eyes dart from me to the rifle I left propped against the doorframe. I know the thoughts going through her head without having to hear them. What kind of living thing could survive gunshot wounds like that and still pull Lucas away? How did it heal itself? Where did it come from? I know what she must think because I've thought the same things.

"Lucas was helping me track it down for a while," I say. "Ever since Shelby came back, it's been following me, and he thought... I guess he thought he could use its connection to me to get close."

"Its connection to you?" Her voice rises, and she drowns her nerves with a long drink from her beer.

Mel's lips move with silent words she never ends up saying as she sits on the floor beside the dog. Hope rests her head against Mel's chest, and the two of them sit there for a while. I don't know what to say to fix this.

I sit at the chair Mel left pulled out from the table and lean against the back of it. I have to explain. Somehow. She deserves an explanation, especially since it's my fault the monster has been stalking her property.

"Lucas's family does that stuff. Hunts monsters." It isn't my place to tell her about his family's job, not my responsibility to tell her about the monster at all, but Mel listens and I don't care about keeping Lucas's secrets anymore. "I know it sounds ridiculous."

"It would if I hadn't just seen it."

The quake in her voice reminds me of how I felt when I first saw it, or when I forced Shelby to transform a little, or when reality finally set in and I couldn't deny the existence of monsters anymore. I never wanted this. I could have gone my whole life only half entertaining the notion of creatures passed down through folklore. Accepting the local lore of the Winter Tree but denying the Icehearts and Bigfoots of the world.

"I need to get to Lucas before it kills him too," I say.

Mel takes another long drink from her beer, draining the can, but doesn't close her eyes to savor the taste. She keeps them wide open, panic-stricken. The whites of them overtaken by crooked fingers of blood vessels swollen from stress.

"You can't. You saw what happened when you shot it."

She shudders at the thought.

"I know where it's going."

I think of what Jasmine told me about skewering the heart with the silver dagger, but I need help.

"You can't be serious. You aren't going up against it alone."

"No, Lucas's mom called in backup. I can lead them to it. I didn't offer at first, didn't tell her I know where it takes its kills, because I didn't want to go."

Mel catches her head in her hands and exhales. "Let them fight it. If they're... if that's what they do. Don't risk your life for this."

I lean forward against the table and hold my fingers over my mouth like a cage. I breathe through them, cold air coming up from my lungs, and try and think of a way to do this without taking them to the cabin myself.

But I can't give them directions, because I don't actually know where the Iceheart is. I only feel it as a vague presence in my chest.

"I don't want to. I really don't," I say.

"Then don't."

"I don't think that's an option anymore. The other hunters... they need what I know, or it'll just keep killing." It will take me as its host and wreak havoc on this town for the rest of the winter.

Mel frowns like she hates the idea of me going out into those woods more than I do.

I have to tell her why I must do this. Then, if I die, at least she'll understand.

"It's Shelby. She is the monster."

My sister is dead.

"She's the monster," Mel repeats. It doesn't sit well with her, what I've said about my sister.

"She's gone. All that's left is the thing she became."

My sister is dead, and I feel nothing.

"Killing the monster will lay her to rest once and for all."

My sister is dead, and I want to live.

FIFTY-TWO

The dread of talking to Jasmine makes the drive feel too short. All the logic leaves my body, and I worry she won't want to help anymore once she knows I could have told her where to find the monster if I had understood the itching feeling in my head. She'll blame me. She'll tell me I should've let the Iceheart take me instead of letting it take the only family she had left.

I sit in her driveway and try to make sense of my racing thoughts. I don't have time for this.

The slam of the truck door echoes in the night, and a light turns on in the front room of Jasmine's house. Her silhouette appears in the doorway before I reach the front step, and she opens the door.

"I was hoping Lucas was with you," she says. "He said he was going to help you."

Guilt consumes me, and I squeeze my eyes shut.

"Have you seen him?"

I can't lie to her.

I'd rather die than tell her the truth.

But I have to live to see the end of this.

"Yeah," I say. "I don't know how he got to where I was, but he was hurt."

Jasmine breathes in violently.

"The Iceheart came for me, and I tried to fight it off. It was going to take me, but Lucas showed up and it took him instead. It didn't want him. But it took him."

Jasmine takes a moment and covers her eyes with her hands, then gestures for me to come inside. She needs me to tell her all the details, and I do. From the way it cut the connection between us for a while before it showed up, to how I needed to protect Mel and the kittens and Hope, to how I knew it didn't want Lucas. I tell Jasmine about how I felt what the Iceheart wanted, then felt how it shifted to need when it took Lucas.

"I know where it is," I say. "I can lead the hunters to it."

"No. Absolutely not."

"I can't tell them where to find the Iceheart, but I feel it. It isn't at the same cabin, because that would be stupid. Please. Let me help."

"I said no, Cara. I can't put you at risk too."

"I'm already at risk. Every day that passes is another chance for it to take me. It's weak now. You know it won't be when it takes me as a new host."

Jasmine rubs her temples. She has to know I'm right. Please let her know that I'm right.

"Let me help. I'll do exactly what you say, just let me show you how to get there. Please."

She rises with the help of her cane and leaves the room. I don't move from where I stand, leaning against the doorframe as if I'm about to leave and figure out how to deal with this on my own. I can't kill it though. Even with the right weapon, I couldn't get to its heart. I almost died alone earlier.

Shit, I need her to let me help. I'm so tired of this. I need it to be done.

"Go home, Cara." Jasmine returns, a phone in her hand.

I open my mouth to argue, but she holds up a hand.

"It's weakest in the afternoon. We will meet here tomorrow and leave at noon. You don't have to do this," she says. "But I appreciate you being willing to try."

Nothing feels like a good response. I could thank her, but it doesn't seem right to be grateful for the chance to walk into a massacre. Instead, I shrug and say, "I'll be glad when it's done."

She looks at me, eyes dark and watery, and I look away. I don't need her to cry. I don't need to be reminded of what Lucas leaves behind if this monster kills him.

I almost wish the Iceheart would give me a sign either way. If he was dead already—I don't know—it would feel okay to wait until tomorrow to leave.

"Go get some rest," Jasmine says. "Go be with your family."

She makes it sound like she thinks I'm going to die. At least she's realistic.

"I haven't slept in weeks," I say.

"You'll learn how," she says. "You learn to live with the fever, and it's almost like there's nothing wrong. Almost."

I take my keys out of my pocket and hook my finger in the keychain—a plastic ear of corn with a smiling face and *Indiana* across the front. Shelby had never been to Indiana, but she thought it was hilarious to have found it in the gift section of a gas station almost a thousand miles from the keychain's home state. The reminder of her aches, but I hold on to it. That's the Shelby I want to remember.

"Are you sure you're going to be all right tonight?" I ask. "Do you want me to stay a bit longer?"

It feels wrong to leave her here all alone with only worries about her son keeping her company.

"No, thank you. I'll see you tomorrow. Drive safe."

I leave, clutching the keychain tight in my good hand as I walk to the truck. The corn comforts me and keeps me from tearing at my skin because Shelby would have done this for me. She would have lived, I think, if things hadn't gone so horribly bad. She would have saved herself out of spite, despite there being nothing left to stay for, so I'll do the same.

FIFTY-THREE

My parents sit at the table, red-eyed, with their phones in their hands and willing the screens to come to life with a phone call or message from someone, anyone. When I come through the door, they look at me, only half relieved. Somehow, I keep forgetting they think she's still alive.

"Have you seen Shelby?" Mom asks. "Heard from her?"

"No. She doesn't talk to me," I say.

Mom frowns and Dad puts a hand on her back. "I thought I heard her leave last night... where would she have gone?" she says, pain lacing her voice. "What is going on with her?"

The handle of Jasmine's dagger digs into my hip, reminding me of its presence. It doesn't bring as much comfort now, because I know, if it comes down to it, I'll have to use it for its intended purpose. As Jasmine said, I'll know exactly whose heart I'm stabbing.

The truth dances on the tip of my tongue, intentionally cruel and miserable.

"I don't know." I don't want to lie anymore. I'm so, so tired of lying.

Mom's shoulders shake for a second before she breaks into violent tears. They spill down her cheeks in waves and collect on the shoulder of Dad's shirt where she buries her face. Is what I'm doing going to fix anything? Or will it be the thing that kills them?

"Lucas is missing too." I don't know why I say it. It doesn't make things any better.

If anything, it makes them worse.

"I don't understand how the police haven't caught the person responsible for this," she mutters.

I could tell them I'll look for her tomorrow because there's a search party going out for Lucas, but I can't risk them keeping me home. I need them to think I'm going out for normal reasons—looking for a new job or doing on schoolwork in the library.

When this is all over, I'll tell them everything I can.

But my parents will not have to live with the idea of their daughter becoming a monster, a killer, a demon. They will remember her as the bright girl she was before she lost herself.

Dad looks at me with sadness mixed in among the dark circles of exhaustion around his eyes. I swear, the last two weeks have made the hair at his temples thin, and grayed what remains. Mom too, though she'd been going gray from stress for a long time.

I hate this.

I hate seeing them like this, broken, beaten down until they shouldn't have any hope left. Maybe they didn't for a while, but Shelby's return lit a spark. It fades now in their eyes, but they try so hard to keep it lit.

"What about you, Cara? Are you okay?" Dad asks. "How are you feeling?"

"I'm cold, but I'm okay." I look down at my boots, scuffed and stained from salt. "Don't worry about me."

"We love you. We can't help worrying," Mom says.

Their words twist in my gut like a knife. I have been lying to my parents for weeks, putting myself in danger, and I can't even tell them what I'm going to do tomorrow. They could lose me too, and I can't even say goodbye the way I want to.

"I'm going to go get some rest, okay?" I say though I'll be up all night. "I'll tell you if she texts me."

They say goodnight and, even though it burns, I hug them each for longer than usual. I don't want this to be the last time, but it could be.

I keep myself together until I get to my room, then I let the tears fall.

After the encounter with the Iceheart, I had to be strong for Mel, then for Jasmine, and now for my parents. But I'm so, so scared of what I have to do, no matter how deeply I know it's what will prevent anyone else from dying.

I lean against the side of my bed and rest my face on my knees, quieting the sobs that come from the deepest part of me. Whatever strength I need to get up onto my bed doesn't exist within me, so I stay on the floor.

Charlie sits on my desk and watches me, skeptical of this person who looks like *her* person but doesn't quite seem right.

I can't say goodbye, not the way I'd like, but I can leave a note with an apology.

The words come unfiltered as I scrawl them out on a piece of notebook paper. They feel like the right words, without betraying Jasmine's trust.

Mom and Dad,

If you're reading this, I'm so sorry. I thought I could help because I got wrapped up in the same thing as Shelby and I learned how to stop it. I can't tell you much, because it isn't my secret to share, but please try and understand that I was doing this for you and I was doing it for me. Even though it was too late for her, I was doing it for Shelby too.

I didn't want to die. I wasn't supposed to. There are professionals for this kind of thing, and I volunteered to help them because I know things you couldn't even believe. I've seen too much, and I need to end it.

But don't blame yourselves, if I'm gone. I didn't want to leave. I only wanted to not be so afraid anymore.

I love you. Take care of Charlie for me.

Love,

Cara

I leave tears on the paper and don't bother to wipe them away. They soak in and make strange patterns in the ink, but otherwise, the note remains legible.

The dim light keeps me company as I tidy up my desk so there's a clear spot to leave the folded note. Charlie doesn't move from her perch, but she keeps staring at me like she wants nothing more than to understand what's wrong.

"I'm sorry, Charlie. I hope you'll realize it's just me. I'm sick, but I'm still me."

I set the paper in the center of the cleared-off desk, and it looks so formal there. So final. It doesn't feel like enough, but it's all I can do, so I curl up on top of my bed with the window cracked beside me. The cold air fills my lungs and makes me feel almost okay, except everything is very much not okay and I don't think it can ever truly be okay again.

FIFTY-FOUR

When the time comes, I pull the truck into Jasmine's driveway beside a huge, black GMC—the kind the secret service drives in action movies, except this one has regular Illinois plates. I expected something different. The SUV is too clean-cut, too normal. People like this are supposed to drive shiny, vintage Impalas with loud, intimidating engines, or maybe a jacked-up truck built for driving through muddy forest paths.

Then again, Jasmine drives a Chrysler, so I guess I can't judge their badassery by the cars they drive.

I knock on the front door once before someone answers.

"You must be Cara," says a lean man no taller than me dressed in all gray.

"That's me. Your escort for today." I cringe at my awkward use of the word *escort*. I wish I could take it back.

"Milo." He offers a hand, which I take after a few seconds of deliberating whether I should let him feel how dead mine are. "Operation commander."

Jasmine must have told him I already know about the

hunters, so he doesn't bother lying. Instead, he reminds me I cannot speak of this mission to anyone other than the people in this room.

Other than Jasmine, there are eight people in her living room. Milo, two other men, and five women. They all wear uniforms of slate-gray outdoor wear.

"So." I don't know what to say. "What's the plan?" I fake confidence in hopes of someone telling me what to do so we can stop standing around and get out there.

"You will have two of my hunters assigned to you for your protection. Under no circumstances are you to leave their side. If they decide you are being uncooperative, they will return you to the vehicles."

I nod.

"When we arrive at the location, you will wait a safe distance away with your assigned hunters until the threat is neutralized and any victims are recovered from the scene."

Recovered. There's that word again. I hate it. I hate it more and more every time I have to hear it.

Jasmine looks away from everyone, and I know it must be because if any victims are recovered, one might be her son. She almost hides it well, but her hand doesn't quite cover her mouth this time. I catch the corner of her lips quivering.

"Are you confident you can lead us there? How many times have you been to the location?" Milo asks.

I hesitate. "Never. It's..." I look to Jasmine, not sure if I should tell Milo the truth.

"She has a connection to it," Jasmine says in a way that dares the other hunters to say something. "It has stalked her for weeks, tormented her, in hopes of making her the next host."

"I think it's luring me to it, so we can use that to our advantage."

"How do we know it isn't a trap?" Milo asks. "How do we know you aren't already the host?"

"Well, first of all, shouldn't you be able to tell if I'm harboring a cannibal spirit?"

"We don't know this isn't a trap," Jasmine says after she shoots me a warning glance. "But we can't let it take a healthier host. We have a chance to strike while it's weak, so we take it."

Well, at least she's realistic.

"I trust Jasmine, and she trusts you—so, fine. You lead us directly there, but let us handle the rest."

"What if she's not there?" I ask.

"She?" Milo asks. Jasmine must have skipped the detail about my sister.

"*It*. The Iceheart. Its current host is a girl around my age," I say.

Milo looks pleased by my knowledge of the host, and, though I know the information makes his job easier, it stings. Would he look at me differently if he knew who the girl is?

"That is very helpful," he says. "Typically, it keeps its host's form until dusk to lower the risk of being seen. Can you tell me what she looks like?"

"A lot like me, but her hair is white."

Milo hooks his thumbs in his pockets, and I noticed a daggerlike mine sheathed in his belt. The light bouncing off the polished, silver handle catches my eye, and, when I look at the others in the room, they all have knives among the other tools they carry. Guns, lengths of rope, batons, things I don't recognize. These people came prepared, and they're only leaving one of two ways: they finish their job, or they die.

"Does anyone have any questions before we move out?" Milo asks the group. "This is a nasty monster. Hopefully, you will not encounter another like it after today."

His people nod in affirmation.

No wonder Lucas had been so bad at this. He pieced together what he thought was enough skill and knowledge to do this job, but seeing these people—he barely scratched the surface. They remind me of a perfectly coordinated sports team with Milo as their captain. They each know their position, know the tools with which they play, and know their individual and group objectives. Nothing exists aside from the game until it ends.

I take in a breath.

And then Milo instructs us to move.

FIFTY-FIVE

Aside from the directions I give, the car is silent as Milo drives. Nobody asks me questions, probably because they don't want to know the answers. I don't mind the silence. I don't want to explain the sickness the Iceheart left in me, or the way the trees have invisible roots hooked around my ankles so they can pull me in. They want me back so I can kill for them, and their grip tightens with every inch closer we get.

They won't let me go this time, not if we fail.

I open the window beside me a crack and take in the cold air that flutters inside. It earns some grumbling from the backseat that threatens to boil over into a full-blown complaint soon. Milo doesn't seem to notice.

"Can you shut that?" one of the guys in the back asks with a tone that suggests I do as he says.

I don't, because whatever he thinks he can do, I've been dealt worse at this point.

"I thought we hunted monsters, not joined forces with them," he says to anyone in the car who will listen. A couple of voices murmur in agreement.

"Take a right here," I say, ignoring the others.

Milo does as I ask.

"Jasmine said there's no guarantee she won't kill us. Why are we taking any chances?"

When Milo doesn't respond, the guy reaches forward until he touches the controls for my window and closes it. I try with all the strength I have not to let it bother me.

"Ryan, knock it off," Milo finally says. "I am giving her the benefit of the doubt due to the urgency of the situation. As my subordinate, I suggest you do the same. Unless you don't think I'm capable of making this decision."

From the corner of my eye, I watch Ryan shrink back into his seat.

"No, sir. I trust your judgment."

I almost laugh at the way his arrogance vanishes as quickly as it came on. Almost. Instead, I open my window again. Wider this time.

When I see the gravel snow-plow turnaround along the left side of the road, I tell Milo to slow down. This is as far as the roads can take us. We need to go into the woods now.

We slide out of the car and into the snow, and a white woman with rosy cheeks stands beside me and zips a heavy coat up to her neck. A soft-looking, gray scarf peeks out from beneath her collar, and she fluffs it up around her jaw and chin.

"Has the Iceheart shown you anything today? Any visions?" she asks.

"No. It knows I know it has Lucas, and I guess that's enough of a threat."

She frowns.

I double-check for the presence of my dagger.

"How much did it show you the other times?" She bites her lip, nervous about my answer.

"Why do you want to know?"

The woman glances away, off into the distance as though something more interesting has caught her attention. A thin, almost indistinguishable line of moisture collects along her bottom eyelids.

"Are you sure you want me to tell you?" I ask. She won't tell me what it's so important to her, but that isn't my business. Maybe she's had experience with this thing before. Maybe she lost someone too.

"Please." Her breath hitches.

"I watched it kill someone." The blood and violence flash behind my eyes. My voice quivers, weak at the thought of claws and teeth tearing into flesh. "I saw everything."

I wish she hadn't reminded me of it. The memories change from what they were into my greatest fear. I see myself killing those people, not the monster. My hands. My teeth. My face coated in blood. The thought makes me pick at my nails, but this time not in search of pain. This time I look for claws.

"You don't want to know more," I say through gritted teeth.

The rest of the group digs through the hard, black cases of weapons in the back of each SUV. They sling heavy guns over their shoulders and check pouches strapped to their belts to ensure they have enough ammunition. One of them sharpens his dagger on a stone, and a few adjust the layers of gray they wear against the frigid weather.

I stand idly to the side, watch, and wait for someone to tell me what to do. With everyone so official in their matching clothes and serious weapons, I feel out of place. Maybe the guy in the car was right and I can't be trusted. Can the Iceheart make me lead them into a trap?

"Cara." Milo waves me over. "You'll be paired with Linnea and Regan."

Linnea is the woman I'd been talking to moments prior with the scarf bundled to her chin. She has since added a black hat pulled over her ears, and wild, blonde curls escape beneath the wool. Her eyes have dried in the short time since we spoke, and their brightness contradicts the drab colors she wears.

Regan is younger—not much older than me—and looks less like a monster hunter and more like a marathon runner. She wears her red hair in a perfect, high ponytail pulled through a headband that covers her ears. Instead of the bulky cargo pants the others wear, she chose heavy-duty hiking tights with a utility belt. There's no doubt in my mind this woman would kick my ass if I so much as stepped out of line.

"You stay with them no matter what happens," Milo says to me, then turns to his hunters. "Your objective is to keep Cara safe."

They nod, then face me. "Ready?" Regan asks, voice gravelly despite what I expected. I don't know what I expected, really.

"Yep."

"Stay close. All you have to do is get us there. That's it." Linnea tugs on her hat in an attempt to cover more of her neck.

"I can do that."

I think so, at least. There's no telling what kind of control the Iceheart has over me. It's dragged me into the woods, made me see things, feel things—what else can it do?

FIFTY-SIX

Linnea, Regan, and I walk at the front of the group, both hunters with their guns ready in case they need them. I have so many questions I want to ask them, and I'd do almost anything to distract me from the sound of footsteps behind me and the inevitability of what lies ahead. But asking seems wrong. It seems like a violation of the trust they've already offered. So I keep my mouth shut.

The woods are too quiet. Even in the dead of winter, there should be some kind of commotion. Birds and squirrels should still be rushing from branch to branch, searching for food or communicating with others like them. The trees should be chattering with their limbs singing songs in the wind.

Everything is silent. Dead.

I pinch myself a few times to be sure this isn't a dream. Lately, I don't trust myself to know the difference between reality and the Iceheart's visions. A sharp pain creeps up my good arm, and tells me this is real.

I wonder if these woods will let me go when this ends. I

avoided them before—feared them, even—but not like this. What else do they hide? What other monsters do the trees keep secret?

The silence grows unbearable, so I break it. "Have you ever seen an Iceheart before?" I ask the hunters, careful not to be too loud.

"No," Regan says. "But I've heard stories."

"When Jasmine called us, half the team was horrified and the other half ready to pack up and get going right then and there," Linnea adds. "A few weeks more, depending on the temperature, and we could have lost it. It could have taken you, if Jasmine's theory is right, and walked you up to the northernmost edge of the boreal forests to avoid the worst of the heat."

"Oh... " So that's what Shelby meant when she told me where she'd been.

In the beats between conversation, our boots crunch too loudly in the snow.

"I had this assignment about a year ago to hunt this creature. We didn't even have a name for it. It was just 'go and figure this out,'" Regan says. "Size of a cougar. Kind of looked like one, until about halfway down its body when its fur turned to scales and ended in a tail like an alligator."

"What did it do?" Either the conversation or Regan keeps me distracted, and I welcome it.

"Drowned people who went out fishing on this lake in Wisconsin. Didn't eat them. Just drowned them." Regan rubs her nose with a gloved hand. "Never did figure out why. There was no pattern in its kills, and nobody had ever seen anything like it. It took me months to catch up to it."

She pauses, and for a moment I think she might be done with her story. But when I look over at her, her lips form a tight line like she's deciding what to say next, or why she started telling this story to begin with.

"I guess my point is that we have information on the Iceheart. Yeah, it's one of the worst, most elusive things in our region, but we know how it works, how it hunts, what it is."

I look around me at trees that look like exact duplicates of ones we passed already.

"What happens to the monsters once you kill them?" I ask.

Regan frowns. "I can't say."

"Sorry," I say. "I didn't mean to overstep."

"It's fine. I'd ask the same thing if I were in your shoes. After all you've seen... " Linnea speaks this time, but trails off before finishing. I wonder if she's thinking about what I told her I saw in my nightmares.

"I wish I could forget what I've seen."

Really, I could live with knowing the Iceheart exists.

What I want is to forget the last couple weeks with Shelby. The way she looked when she transformed that night, the way she acted before I knew she was the monster, the dinner plate she threw at my face. I wish I could forget trusting Lucas and the feeling of betrayal he left hanging over me.

"Me too," Linnea finally says. "But those things will fade. Eventually, this will all feel shaky as a dream you forget as soon as you wake up."

The conversation falls into a lull. There is still so much to see. So much for me to want to forget, and I don't even know what it'll be like yet. I don't want to watch as my sister shifts into the Iceheart. The thought of what it must look like for her to shift completely makes me dizzy. The eyes and teeth were bad enough.

The Iceheart's pull on me gets stronger with every step. At first, it was a whisper just far enough that I couldn't make out the words. Now it is a siren. It is wailing. It is desperate. I follow it as it tugs on me, like maybe I don't have a choice in whether I keep moving.

I am not ready for this.

I force myself to stop, just to see if I can. My legs tingle with the restless urge to move, but I fight it.

"Are you okay?" Regan asks.

She and Linnea stop beside me, weapons pointed at the ground. Regan's hand tenses, not trusting me. No, not trusting the thing controlling me. I don't blame her.

"Yeah, I'm fine."

The need to keep walking becomes unbearable, so I let go of myself. I count the footsteps I take until I lose hold of my thoughts. Nothing—not the hunters' stories of past monsters, not where I'm leading these people, not my sister's inevitable shift—remains in my head for a little while.

Reality returns as something other than trees comes into view. Something less solid than the last cabin, with one wall collapsed and the ceiling caving in. The windows have all been broken, and two of the three steps to the open front door have rotted through.

I close my eyes and force myself to be still because I know what comes next. One of the people I brought here will kill the Iceheart.

"There it is," I say.

At least I don't have to be the one to do it, won't have to use this dagger against my own family. I imagine pushing the blade through the protective ice around the heart it stole and am glad I didn't come here alone. I don't think I could do it.

"You can't miss it."

They definitely will *not* miss it.

Even if it weren't the only human-made structure within a mile, even if it weren't the only thing ahead of us, they couldn't overlook the thing pacing before it.

Because despite the early hour and the sun shining through a filter of somber clouds, the monster has already begun transforming—Shelby into the Iceheart. Her eyes have been replaced by the Iceheart's, and they burn deep in her eye sockets. Then there's her mouth. She's shifted enough that the pale, scarred skin has stitched together over the sharpened teeth behind her lips.

She paces around the front of the cabin. Back and forth. Back and forth.

"She's so young," Linnea says.

I would give anything to feel something other than the paralyzing nausea gripping my stomach, but seeing my sister only makes me sick.

"Only for now," I say. She doesn't need to know any more.

My sister—the Iceheart—notices me here in a matter of seconds and fixes her gaze on the trees that camouflage our exact position. She knows I'm close. There will be no hiding from her, no safety in the cover of forest.

The others catch up to us, and Milo reminds Linnea and Regan to stay back and keep watch over me. In the last second before they walk into the clearing, Milo orders me not to try anything. My job has been done. All I have left to do is wait.

"Good luck, y'all," Regan says.

In silence, I watch the six of them lift their weapons and march toward the cabin. They make no attempt to sneak up on Shelby, and she stops pacing by the door to lock those bloody eyes on a group I was not supposed to bring.

My pulse spasms as the scene unfolds before me. They surround her from different angles, circling her with guns pointed.

The monster squares up against the hunters, but what remains of my sister doesn't look like much of a threat. Even with some of its features making her more terrifying than usual, the hunters outnumber her and half of them stand at least a head taller. The time she was gone ate away at her muscles and left her too thin. Frail, even. She looks like a strong enough wind could blow her halfway to Chicago.

The hunters stop before they get too close, and leave twenty feet between them and her. Milo gestures for them to spread out, and they do so without taking their eyes off the girl in front of them.

What does this look like from their point of view?

I can't dream of a world where anyone gets used to seeing things like this, seeing the victims like Shelby and all the others. Monsters, I could deal with. But I could never get used to the wreckage they leave behind.

The Iceheart takes a step forward, closer to the hunters. Its movement makes them retreat a little and lift their weapons higher.

I am going to have to watch them destroy this beast and, with it, my sister.

This is it.

One of the hunters lifts her weapon and fires a warning shot. The bullet tears into the Iceheart's thigh, and dark blood blooms across the torn jeans clinging to my sister's legs. A screech like winter wind ripping off the trees escapes as the scar over Shelby's mouth bursts open with a spray of blood and skin.

Her body contorts in a gruesome interpretive dance, and I realize what's happening too late to shield my eyes from it.

The transformation stretches her limbs, forcing her to stand taller in the snow on unnaturally long legs. Jagged, gray bones push their way out of her fingertips, mangle the decaying gray skin and make her nails fall to the ground. She tightens her hands into fists against the pain of changing forms, and the tendons and muscles in her body tense to the point of snapping. Her clothes tear and fall in shreds to the snow, leaving nothing covering the rotten body of a nightmare.

I thought watching her die would be the worst thing I'd have to see.

I was wrong.

FIFTY-SEVEN

A minute passes before no trace of Shelby remains, but it feels like a decade of watching her body pull itself apart and rearrange itself.

I catch my balance on a nearby tree.

Blood from the newly opened wound on its face trickles down its chin and spills onto its chest, collecting in the deep crevices between ribs. Even from here, streaks of fresh red contrast against the pale gray skin stretched over her bones.

Regan and Linnea watch in horror as the scene unfolds before us. We're supposed to stay here and be quiet until the end, but I can't stand here defenseless. I pull the dagger from its leather sheath and clutch it in my right hand. The silver catches in the light, and Linnea notices.

"Where'd you get that?" she asks in a whisper.

Regan turns, eyes wide.

I ignore them both.

The second shot erupts from the end of another hunter's gun. It lodges in the soft space between one of the Iceheart's ribs. The monster reacts by swiping at the hunters with one of its arms, and the clawed hand at the end hits one of them in the skull with a sickening crack. It sends him soaring across the clearing, where he lands in a heap.

Gunfire erupts around me as the hunters try and inflict enough damage to slow the thing down.

In the second that passes before I get my eyes back on the remaining hunters, another hits the ground closer to me. I make the mistake of looking too closely at how the bone protrudes from the side of her leg, and my head spins.

"I'll be okay back here," I say. "You could go help them."

Milo and his three remaining hunters take cover behind anything they can find—tree trunks, stacks of wood, the edge of the cabin—and take more shots at the monster's rapidly healing body. It recovers faster than it did yesterday, and I don't let myself think about where it found the energy.

"We have our orders," Linnea says.

Regan looks like she wants to go and help her team.

"Your orders have already gotten two people hurt." I won't say *killed*. I can't. "That's a quarter of the team down in minutes."

"Cara, we can't disobey him," Linnea insists. "He's the boss. He calls the shots."

I fiddle with the dagger in my hand, looking for the right thing to say to get Linnea to listen to me.

"Maybe she's right, Lin," Regan says.

Regan has set herself away from me and Linnea to help the hunter at the treeline.

"We need more heat on this monster," Regan says. "Milo's not doing so great out there. Michelle will keep an eye on Cara." She turns to the dark-skinned woman who, despite having a bone sticking out of her leg and sweat streaming down her face, still points her weapon at the monster. "Right, Michelle?"

"I'm not going anywhere else," Michelle says without taking her eyes off the monster. She deposits a few rapid-fire bullets into its side while Regan and Linnea argue over what to do.

"The bullets aren't even slowing it down? How are we supposed to get close enough to use the daggers?" A bit of fear laces Linnea's voice. She doesn't believe we can kill this thing.

I cradle the weapon Jasmine gave me in my hands like something precious.

I don't want to do this.

"If you can help the others slow it down… " My eyes meet Regan's, then Linnea's. "I want to be the one to do it."

Blood in my ears leaves even my own voice sounding miles away, and I worry I might miss their response.

I want to hand the weapon over to Linnea or Regan. Anyone who will take it, I'll give it to them gladly.

But they won't. They have their own daggers.

I don't *really* want to do this.

"We're professionals. We trained for this," Linnea says. Regan nods in agreement.

The handle of the dagger grounds me as I tighten my hand around it. I've never found comfort in a weapon like I find comfort in this.

And, distracted by a constant wave of bullets hitting its body, the Iceheart has lost control of me. For now. I need to take advantage of this.

"No, you don't understand," I insist. "I didn't want to do this at first, but the girl you saw before it shifted? She was my sister. I watched it destroy her. So I want to destroy it."

The three women share wide eyes and looks of horror mixed with sympathy.

"No way. I'm sorry, but no. We are not putting you in that position," Linnea says.

"I've been in worse," I say. "Just, cover me. Please."

The hunters deliberate, mostly rattling off reasons why they should not allow me to help. Regan wants to help her team, Linnea seems to think the three of us might be the only ones to get out of this. Michelle leans back against a tree, still shooting.

Another hunter goes down, leaving Milo and two others.

We watch as the monster goes for the body and feeds on the still-warm remains, desperately trying to regain energy lost in healing and fighting.

"Okay fine," Linnea says. Her face goes gray as she tries not to look at the creature devouring her colleague. "Fine. Milo is going to be pissed. But fine, you can help."

"Pissed is better than dead," Regan says.

With the backdrop of gunfire from Milo and the others, the four of us create a new plan. Regan and Linnea will rush out, fingers on the trigger and raining bullets on the creature's corpselike body. I'll wait in the trees, safely guarded by Michelle, until the monster falls. Then I approach, dagger in hand.

For Shelby. For Jasmine. For everyone who lost anyone to this monster.

I'll tear its heart out.

For the next moments, I erase Shelby from my memories and lie to myself that the monster has only ever been this form. A beast. An abomination. It needs to be put down.

Regan and Linnea move out with their weapons drawn

and firing, burying bullets in the decayed skin of the Iceheart from a different angle than Milo and the others. Only the first man to be hit stayed down, so we have seven guns against one monster.

This has to be enough.

The Iceheart backs away, trapped against the outer wall of the cabin. Chunks of its flesh come off when bullets hit, and it doesn't heal as fast as before, as fast as it did when we got here. Blood the color of withered roses blooms over its colorless limbs, and the torn skin remains jagged like the mouth it gnaws through every day.

This will work.

This has to work.

Surely Milo supplied his team with enough bullets for this. He had to have known it wouldn't go down so easily.

I pray to everything. I pray to nothing—whatever decides to listen—that the hunters have enough for this to work.

The monster falls to a knee in the snow, and I take that as my cue to emerge from the safety of the trees. With every step I take, I envision the exact spot where I saw its heart when I shot it with Mel's gun. From here, the edges of an organ encased in ice a glacial shade of blue show through one of its many wounds.

The frozen heart it stole shines bright in its chest.

I clutch the dagger so tight, it becomes a part of my hand, an extension of one limb in the absence of the other.

The shooting continues.

The monster doesn't rise.

"Cara, get out of here," Milo demands as he reloads his weapon.

"No," I say. "Keep shooting."

The Iceheart throws its head back to the sky and opens

shriveled lungs into the kind of scream you hear at night coming from the woods, the kind that renders you unable to move, to breathe, to fall back asleep. The corners of its mouth tear open farther with how its jaw seems to unhinge, and I'd swear I could hear the sound of skin ripping.

It calls for its pack.

They won't get here in time. I won't let them.

FIFTY-EIGHT

Milo looks at Linnea and Regan, questioning, then back at me. He may be the professional, but I've hijacked his mission. And we're doing this whether he likes it or not.

He gives the others hand gestures I assume mean move closer, because everyone takes a few steps forward while still pulling their triggers.

I follow two steps behind and keep my eyes on the Iceheart. Decay consumes its body even more so than before now that the skin has broken and exposed bones. One of the bullets has shattered the ribcage guarding its heart, leaving me with a clean opening to guide the dagger in.

"Aim for its chest," Milo instructs the hunters.

The group stops walking when we are within feet of the monster.

With every violent strike of silver bullets against the thick casing of ice, the cracks grow deeper. Shards of the glistening shell fall away from the edges and smash against the ground.

I don't think of anything but that heart. The cracks like canyons give me a place to dig the blade in. They will let me pry away at the ribcage until it no longer protects the vulnerable organ beneath.

My ears ring from the sound of guns firing on either side of me, and I spare a moment to imagine how foolish I must look standing here with this knife among shooters.

In this cold, there should not be the putrid stench of rot, but it fills the air around me. It thickens in my nose and throat and chokes me, growing stronger with every step closer to our enemy.

The skin that, from a distance, looked only stretched and dried, is broken in places with scabs and sores. Combined with the missing pieces stolen by bullets, the monster looks like carrion half eaten by scavengers of the forest.

Some of its wounds already curl at the edges, each side of the opening returning to the other in an attempt to heal, but the damage is too great. The constant destruction imposed on the monster slows the process of recovery.

"Cara, now," Milo says. He holds a hand up to stop the others from shooting, and they lower their weapons.

I lift my weapon in a fist, pinky finger against the guard before the blade, and step forward until I don't need to anymore.

Those eyes make my pulse race. Somewhere behind them—no. No, I won't think about anything but this disgusting thing kneeling in front of me.

I am the executioner today.

This thing will die for what it has done, and it will be at my hand.

For Shelby.

A thin layer of ice around its heart crackles as it slowly

heals over the soft tissue, and I watch the damage smooth over in the places where it isn't so bad. Time has already begun to run out before this thing recovers again and takes the opportunity to tear into me as I stand mere inches from it.

Still, I want to say something to mark the significance of this moment. It makes me want to offer some kind of last words to my sister, if she's even still in there.

But I don't.

I take in a breath, hold it in my lungs.

Then I plunge the dagger into the monster's still-beating heart. For a little while, the muscles pulse beneath the pressure of the blow and push syrupy blood out over my hand.

Heat collects in my stomach just beneath my ribs. The burning feeling spreads from that spot to my chest, my legs, but remains hottest in my abdomen. My own heart pumps boiling blood through me to the farthest ends of my body. Even the arm I thought I'd lost regains a little feeling, but not enough to use it to add power to my attack.

"Cara!" The voice belongs to no one. They sound so far away.

I push the blade in deeper but the dagger's guard stops it from going any farther in, so I twist, drawing more blood out of the Iceheart's chest and onto my hands. Its mouth gapes in shock, exposing all those gory needlelike teeth.

I thought I'd feel something.

Hands find my shoulders, but I don't turn to see who they belong to. My eyes remain on the monster's face as it gradually goes lifeless. Its head hangs forward, forehead against my own but I don't care, and its limbs sag without the power of the soul to keep them tight.

The heat in my body pulls my focus in and out. The

corners of my vision turn black and fade at the edges. Beneath me, the forest floor sways and makes me sick.

I look down to the burning in my stomach and find the source of it. Not fire, but four of the monster's bone claws. They disappear into the flesh beneath my ribcage, covered in blood. My blood.

FIFTY-NINE

Commotion swirls around me, too fast for me to register the movement and sounds of people panicking.

My hands fall to the claws dug into my stomach, and the monster's dead body slumps forward against me. The weapons at the end of its fingers dig deeper into the softest parts of my abdomen. Pain erupts through my body. Every inch of me bursts into flame, hot agony in my bones and my blood.

I breathe in the scent of death.

A cloud of voices hangs around me, but I don't decipher any of what they say.

I have to get these claws out of me.

I can't die here too.

Only the fingers on my right hand close around the foreign limb embedded in me—my left feels more like a phantom limb than usual. The Iceheart's skin is rough, its hand bony.

"No! Don't," someone says.

I don't listen.

But the claws will not come loose.

Hands appear on my shoulder, too warm, and stop me from tearing at the last thing tethering me to this monster.

"You can't," the voice says. Milo. There are three of him hovering over me. "We don't know what those claws are holding together inside of you. You could bleed out."

As if on cue, I cough up sticky blood. It bubbles out from my lungs and dribbles down my chin.

Oh god, my parents.

I can't die.

I can't let them lose both their daughters without so much as a goodbye.

I should have left them more than a note.

"Help is on the way," Milo says. "Just hang on a bit longer."

My eyelids droop, heavy from exhaustion, and my body wobbles slightly with the earth moving beneath it. A wave of nausea hits me hard, levels me.

They think I went to the library.

They think Shelby's the only one they need to worry about today.

But Shelby's dead now.

In the last moments before the darkness at the edges of my vision closes in on me, I wish I'd told them the truth. I wish I told them Shelby was already dead. I wish I told them I was on my way out, sickness in my blood and bad ideas in my head.

The Iceheart started digging my grave the day I hit it with my truck.

And I walked right into the hole it made for me.

"Stay awake, Cara. You need to hold on." Milo's voice has too many layers, reverberating through my head and shaking my brain until it turns to liquid.

I can't.

My eyes only process blurry versions of the scenery behind the monster weighing down on me. A vignette of shadow frames the view, creeping in until no light gets through.

Milo keeps talking and I try to hang onto the words and stay awake, but I want so badly to sleep. My eyes sting from the dry air and the salt in my tears, I want to shut them. I need to rest. Blood gurgles in my lungs, collecting in a pool where there should be air. My breaths grow shallow until I have to remind myself to breathe.

He wants me to hold on. I want to hold on.

But I let go.

SIXTY

Hungry trees and monsters surround me in the darkness—miniature Icehearts, demons of skin and bones, nightmares I can reach out and touch. They let their bone claws and teeth dance over my frozen body, leaving intricate patterns in the layer of frost on my skin, but they never draw blood. Fear renders me unable to move, to breathe, and the last air I took into my lungs is all I have to survive on. What little oxygen I stole runs thin already, but I cannot take any more.

The monsters don't let me relax my broken body while they inspect their kill, inspect me.

Hot, sticky fluid the consistency of syrup trails down my chin and chest, and tongues touch my neck for a taste of the blood bubbling up from my lungs and out my burning throat.

If my mouth weren't so full of liquid, if I could breathe, I would scream. But instead, I suffocate, I drown.

They hold me down.

They whisper to me.

They tell me I can rest now.

They use Shelby's voice to tell me they will take away my pain, they will take away the chill in my core. I only have to let them have me.

"No." I choke on the metallic pool of blood in my mouth. With the word, more spills down my chin and entices the tongues of monsters who've gone so long with a sick hunger rotting them from the inside out. "I'd rather die."

I'd rather die.

I'm going to die.

SIXTY-ONE

I lie on my back on a stiff bed about as comfortable as I imagine the metal tables of a morgue to be, and the thought sends a shiver through me. The left side of my body tingles like it doesn't belong to me anymore, like my mind hovers outside and watches me from above. When I try to move, my limbs don't respond to the command. Even my eyelids remain still as stone when I try to open them.

I must be dead.

Or most of the way through dying.

The metallic taste of blood coats my tongue along with the sour sting of bile, and I can't wash it away in all my attempts to swallow. It tastes like the smell of rot that emanated from the Iceheart, and I wonder if the decay has already taken hold of my insides.

"She's waking up." A hopeful and familiar voice comes wrapped in echoes from somewhere far from me.

Are they talking about me?

Am I coming back from the dead?

I search my body for a sign I'm alive—a prickle, a touch of warmth, anything. Even pain would do.

There is nothing.

"Cara? Please... please get up." I know this voice. I recognize the way it rises at the end of my name in a question, then how it falls to a near whisper when she pleads with what's left of me to wake.

The voice makes me want to leave the place where I lie unconscious so I won't die with the agony within it being the last thing I hear.

What happened to me?

I remember monsters crawling over every inch of my body. I remember blood in my lungs, my mouth, spilling down the front of me.

"Please," she says.

Someone sniffles and fails to hold back a tremor of a sob. Where am I?

We faced it. The Iceheart. People whose faces blur in my memory until their features fade completely had followed me into the woods.

The sound of bullets resonates in my memory. So many bullets. We must have thrown thousands of dollars of silver into the monster's body to slow it down.

A finger on my right hand twitches, an involuntary moment. Heat spreads up my arm from my fingertips, and the limb shies away out of reflex.

"What are you doing?" Another speaker, male, directs his voice at someone else. The weight of worry drags each syllable down on its way out. "You're going to burn her!"

"The heat should wake her." Another voice, an unfamiliar one.

The cold in me lives on. A chill like death infects every

cell in my body and reminds me that the Iceheart's fever hasn't faded.

"Stop," the first voice pleads. "She doesn't need more pain."

"She shouldn't have been out there with your people. She's here because you put her in danger," the male voice says, level but livid.

Silence follows.

Everything floods back to me.

I didn't just lead the hunters to the monster like I'd planned. I stood before it with a silver dagger clenched in my fist. They brought it to its knees and exposed its vulnerabilities so I could prey upon them.

My palm didn't even sweat around the metal when I made my move.

There was nothing ceremonious about the kill.

Heat consumes my arm, then my shoulder, then the entire right side of my body. Beads of sweat collect on my face and collarbone, pooling in the dip above my sternum.

Lights sear my eyes when they snap open and I wake for no other reason than to get away from the source of the heat.

"Cara!" Dad's hands fall to my shoulders to keep me from tearing at the tubes and wires I've been connected to. When I calm down, he turns to one of the blurry faces from my memory. Even with clear features now, I can't quite place him.

"Thank god you're okay," Mom cries. "What were you thinking, going out there like that? You could have been killed."

"I wasn't." At least, I don't think so. Maybe there's still a chance I might not live.

"Do you have any idea what we would've..." Her

composure shatters before she can finish. "Do you know what we would have done if we lost you too? Your father and I wouldn't have been able to go on."

"You could have asked us for help, Cara. You shouldn't have done this alone." Dad speaks in a low voice to hide his frustration and disappointment, byproducts of his fear.

"I didn't know how to tell you," I say. "I didn't think you'd believe me."

When I speak, pain shoots up the left side of me and dies at my shoulder. I arch my back in response to it and shut my eyes tight against tears blooming in the corners. A new kind of fire erupts inside of me, and I don't recognize it as my normal response to even the dullest heat. No, this fire comes from pain.

A flash of memory crosses behind my eyes.

The monster's claws. The soft area beneath my ribs.

Blood coating the bones broken through its fingertips, coating the shirt beneath my jacket.

"What happened to me?"

My parents can convince me I'll be okay. They can convince me I won't die from this, even if it's a lie. I don't care if it's a lie.

"The Iceheart is dead," the blurry-faced guy says.

A little sob escapes Mom's throat. She meant to hide it from me with a hand over her mouth. They don't know if I'll be okay. Nobody does. They won't lie to me for fear the shake in their voices will give them away.

"You have lacerations to your liver and kidneys, a collapsed lung, internal bleeding, broken ribs. You've been asleep for two weeks. Your body can't take any more right now."

My head spins. Lacerations. Collapsed lung. Internal

bleeding. Broken bones. I don't know where to begin processing what he's said.

"Where am I?"

"A special hospital in Fargo."

I breathe. I've never been out of Minnesota. The realization overwhelms me, though I am probably only mere miles from the borders of the state that couldn't protect me.

Mom looks around the room, and I follow her gaze to sterile rows of vials and medical supplies lined up on metal shelves. The light that felt so aggressive on my eyes earlier is actually dimmer than I thought and comes from a lamp that leaves the room cast in a soothing glow.

"Lucas's mom told us everything," Dad says. "The public gets a different story, though. Serial killer."

He doesn't like the decision but accepts it.

"They weren't going to tell us. Jasmine broke protocol by telling us. The poor woman... "

I look at Mom when she trails off, and I already know why she stopped speaking. I don't want to know where her sentence will lead.

She has more gray in her hair today. New lines in her skin appear beside her frown and at the corners of her lightless eyes. Dad doesn't look much better. He runs a hand over the receding hairline I've now contributed to.

"Did they find Lucas?" Nobody has mentioned him since I woke up. Why is nobody talking about him?

Mom looks away, folding her arms over her stomach and hunching over in her chair. The words she doesn't say serve as an answer to my question.

My chest constricts, and the machines beside me start beeping frantically. Too many emotions flood my head, and I can't process the agony, panic, and distress of knowing the truth. I try to tell myself he deserved to die for lying to me, for putting himself in such a thoughtless situation, but I can't.

Nobody deserves what he got.

A woman dressed in scrubs rushes to my bedside with a syringe in one hand. She injects the contents into one of the tubes attached to me, and, gradually, I find the panic fading into a dull discomfort.

I sink into the soft clutches of whatever drug she gave me to calm down.

"I understand you have a lot to talk to her about, but please be careful not to upset her," the woman says.

Dad nods, understanding spread across his face.

"She isn't out of the woods yet," the woman says. Clearly, she doesn't know what the woods mean to me now.

SIXTY-TWO

Shelby comes home in a box this time, but it still doesn't contain a body. We tell people the box contains ashes to be buried in the town cemetery set along the main road on the way into town.

I can't focus on the service given by someone who thinks my sister died at the hands of a serial killer. Everyone here except me and my parents and Mel has been fed a lie about my sister's death and the events leading up to me having to rely on an intricate, wooden walking stick to get around.

I'm sick of lies.

"Are you okay?" Mom asks in a whisper.

I hold the symbolic little box tight to my chest with my trustworthy arm, afraid I'll drop it in the process of handing it to my parents.

"Yeah," I say, ignoring how scratchy the wool coat I wear in place of my ruined leather one makes my skin.

The jacket wasn't the only thing that couldn't be fixed, but the hunters' medics patched me up as best as they could. They taught me to use my left arm a little despite it being rendered useless from the fever, and how to walk again after they rebuilt my insides.

The cold in me won't go away, and neither will the limp in my step from the damage the monster's claws did.

The speaker, a retired pastor, concludes the service with an awkward prayer Shelby would have hated, then asks the handful of folks in attendance for thoughts and strength for my parents and me.

My parents lower the box into the ground in the center of the cemetery, farthest from the trees, and I take a red rose from a stack of them. The florist must have meant to cut the thorns off, but they missed one on the flower I took. It draws blood from the thumb on my dead hand, and the bright bead stands out so violently against my pale skin.

It reminds me of the feeling of the Iceheart's syrupy blood felt as it flowed over my hand, the feeling of the dagger pulsing in my hand as the monster's heart beat for the last time.

I move toward the hole in the frozen Earth and deposit my rose on what remains of my sister.

"I'm sorry," I whisper so the surrounding forest won't hear. "I'm sorry I couldn't save you."

EPILOGUE

People get really weird about the fact that I survived a serial killer. For some awful reason, they want details. They want the play-by-play account of my experience like I'm their own local true-crime podcast.

I think I actually preferred the community thinking I *was* the serial killer. At least then they left me alone.

Mel drives her Subaru past the edge of the county and I sit in the passenger's seat, trying to understand what her GPS wants us to do. We have a mama cat and her kittens to trap behind a dollar store an hour from Wolf Hill, but the drive might take longer since half the roads on Mel's old device don't exist anymore.

"There." I point to a sign for a junction in a few miles. "We turn there and go, uh, probably north? We'll figure that out in a minute."

Mel laughs but follows my instructions instead of those of the GPS, which has begun recalculating again. Eventually, the empty back roads give way to a small downtown strip in a town I forgot the name of. Tucked behind a fast-food coffee chain, I see the dollar store. Or, I see *a* dollar store. Then, a little ways ahead, I see another. This town is, like many around here, too small for a Wal-Mart, so it compensates by having three different discount stores.

"It's the other one," Mel says as she passes the first.

My phone buzzes in my hand, and I glance at the preview of the text. An unknown number sent a photo of the Iceheart's tree, withered and collapsed now that the burden of the monster's preservation has been lifted. A heap of bark, probably still carved with the initials of those who visited it, remains in the center of its clearing.

It's gone.

I delete the message and focus back on the task at hand.

This is our first litter since Paisley and her siblings were adopted, and a little nervousness lingers in my mind. Mel told me what to expect—the cats will be scared, probably filthy, maybe injured, and might hiss or scratch—but that isn't what worries me. I still think about the day Charlie forgot who I was, and how much it hurt. What if these kittens are extra afraid of me because of what I am now? What if I can't work with animals because I'm part monster?

Even Jasmine told me not to think like that, but it creeps in despite all efforts to fight it.

"There's Mama," Mel says.

I follow her gaze to a skinny gray tabby just before the cat disappears into a tipped-over cardboard box. Mel inches closer with her trap, keeping an eye on the box where the cat went. We work quickly to set the trap's triggers and put food in the very back. At the scent of the canned food I crack open, Mama peers cautiously beneath one of the box's flaps.

"She seems friendly," I say. "Or hungry."

The two of us go back to the car where Hope waits

politely in the backseat and give the cat time to investigate. If we're lucky, Mama will go in first and we'll be able to swoop in and grab the kittens. If not, we could be here for a while.

From where I sit, I catch sight of Mama as she emerges from her hiding place. She looks around, then sets her head low as she makes a run for the food. Through the open window of the car, I hear the trap snap shut.

"That was easy," Mel says. "Here's hoping the kittens are in that box, so we can head out."

My side aches as I walk back to where we left the trap—the pain shows up sometimes, a reminder of how close to death I came. Mama sounds unhappy about being trapped away from her kittens and growls at Mel as she gets closer to the trap. I pick up a smaller carrier and go to the box to see if there's anyone inside.

I find three balls of fur, eyes and ears still shut, in the far back corner. They look only a few days old and only squirm a little when I reach in and pick them up.

Either way, they'd be freaked out by strange hands and strange smells coming into their home, so I realize this might be exactly the right thing for me to do. Between this and working the reception desk at the clinic where Mel works as a vet tech, I tend to forget how much I cared about Nice-N-Spice.

With the three kittens snuggled into the blanket-lined carrier, I meet Mel at the corner of the building where she waits with Mama.

"I told you it would be fine," she says.

Mel looks kind of smug, so I roll my eyes. Though I guess there are worse endings than Mel being right.

ACKNOWLEDGMENTS

There are so many people who have helped make this book what it is today that I'd like to thank. First and foremost, my wonderful friend and editor Briana Morgan for believing in Cara's story and encouraging me to put it out into the world. I may not be writing this without you! For my critique partners, Jenny Howe and Courtney Kae, thank you for reading TIHOT and sending both constructive feedback and cheerleading along this book's nearly five-year-long journey. Thank you to my early readers: Scott Moses, Shayla Diana, Renee Reynolds, and Lindsay Hess for the enthusiasm, support, and feedback. A huge thank you to my 2018 PitchWars mentor, Jessica Bayliss, for choosing me and this book to mentor through a rigorous and fast-paced couple of months right in the middle of a very chaotic time in my life.

Of course, I'd also like to thank my family for supporting my interest in writing horror instead of "nice happy stories" even if they don't always get it. Special thanks to my sister, Heather, for reading an early copy and leaving a review, and to my brother, Matthew, for answering culinary questions like "is bone marrow slurpable?" Thank you to my boyfriend for letting me bounce increasingly unhinged thoughts off you at weird hours of the night.

There are so many other folks who have supported me through this journey to put TIHOT out into the world, and, if you don't see your name here, blame my bad memory. I appreciate everyone who has supported me and this story on our journey to publication.

TIHOT is a story of loss and of learning to let go of a person who isn't the same one you used to love, be it a family member, a partner, or a friend. It's about trusting yourself to know what's best for you, and about finding your way in a world where the odds are stacked against you. I hope it resonates with people in a similar boat to Cara, trying to do what they think they have to just to make a future for themselves. You've got this. It gets easier.

About the Author

Samantha Eaton is a horror author and animal advocate living in the woods of midcoast Maine with her three rescue cats, three rescue dogs, and an ever-fluctuating flock of chickens. When she isn't writing or reading horror, she's hiking, traveling, taking glamour shots of the aforementioned animals, gently traumatizing her loved ones with heavy music, or participating in other ADHD-driven nonsense.

 twitter.com/Samantha_Eaton3

 instagram.com/seaton611